VANISHED

DI SARA RAMSEY
BOOK 26

M A COMLEY

To my mother, gone but never forgotten. Miss you every second of every day, Mum.

Also to my dear friend, Mary, I hope you found the peace you were searching for, lovely lady.

ACKNOWLEDGMENTS

Special thanks as always go to @studioenp for their superb cover design expertise.

My heartfelt thanks go to my wonderful editor Emmy, my proofreaders Joseph and Barbara for spotting all the lingering nits.

A special shoutout to all my wonderful ARC Group, who help to keep me sane.

PROLOGUE

The rain was relentless. After a heavy shower, it had now lessened to a soft drumming against the windows of the sleek modern house, nestled on the outskirts of Stretton Sugwas in Hereford. The house had a stark white exterior. It was a detached property, one of six executive homes on the estate. Inside, it really came to life with its glass-panelled walls and minimalist decor, which was a testament to the life Jessica and Daniel Harding had built together—perfect, ordered and untouchable. Underneath all that, the tension was palpable.

Standing in the kitchen, Jessica looked out of the bi-fold doors at her beautifully landscaped garden, delighted to have finally found a gardener who could bring her vision to life. Her hands came to rest on her stomach, and the dread she'd kept at bay hit her with full force. She closed her eyes, hoping her fear would subside. She hadn't told him yet. The pregnancy had come as a shock. She'd bought ten of those expensive pregnancy kits, and each one had revealed the same answer. A twist in her life that she hadn't envisioned or been prepared for. The trouble was that this wasn't the only secret she was keeping from Daniel.

She swayed, mimicking the grasses beyond the patio as they

moved in the breeze. Caught up in her thoughts, it took her a while to realise that her phone was vibrating across the worktop behind her, disrupting the silence she was holding close. She made no attempt to answer it, didn't even turn to look at it. She already knew who it would be. Paul. His text messages had been non-stop since their last meeting. He'd made it clear that he wanted her, wanted much more from their relationship. Instead of stolen moments, he wanted to devote quality time to her. The results of the tests had changed all of that. Jessica didn't want more. She'd admitted to herself that she'd made a terrible mistake, and now the consequences were rippling through her in ways she hadn't expected.

The phone stopped, only to ring a second time, then a third and fourth. Finally, the caller gave up—except they didn't. The phone tinkled to let her know that a message had been sent instead.

She clenched her jaw, trying to block out the noise, but guilt surged through her. She picked it up and glanced at the screen. His message was brief, but the tone was unmistakable.

We need to talk. You can't avoid this forever. Is it his or mine?

An icy shiver trickled down her spine. Her gaze flicked towards the front door as if expecting Daniel to walk in at any moment. She had kept the affair from him, hidden it well—or so she thought. But she'd had her doubts lately because something had changed with Daniel recently. He had grown distant from her, secretive even. He hadn't come right out and confronted her, but Jessica sensed something was lurking beneath the surface.

A knock on the front door startled her, and she jumped. She quickly shoved her phone in her pocket and composed herself. It wasn't Daniel; he wouldn't knock—he'd use his key. Heart racing, Jessica took tentative steps across the marble floor that they had imported from Italy at an exorbitant cost.

Opening the door, she exhaled a large breath at the sight of her best friend, Laura. Jessica instantly guessed that something was wrong. Laura's features were usually full of warmth and energy, but today she seemed pale and worried.

"Jess," Laura began. She stepped into the hallway before Jessica had the chance to invite her in. "We need to talk."

Jessica had a flashback to Paul's message, and she shuddered and closed the door behind her, nerves already tightening her stomach. "What's going on?" she asked, trying to keep the panic out of her voice.

Without removing her shoes, a bugbear of Jessica's, especially on a foul day like today, Laura tore through to the lounge and sank into the luxurious sofa. Anxiously, she wrung her hands together. She hesitated before speaking. "I know this is going to be hard to hear, but... I think Daniel knows. About the affair... or should I say, *your* affair?"

The statement floored Jessica. Flabbergasted by her friend's announcement, she lowered herself into the seat beside Laura, momentarily rendered speechless as her mind raced at warp speed. Her eyes widened, and all she could do was stare at her friend. Finally, she found her voice and stammered breathlessly, "What— what do you mean? How could he know?"

Laura reached for her hand and looked her in the eye, her expression a mix of sympathy and unease. "He popped in to see a mate of his in the office last week. I overheard them talking when I was putting some files away. He didn't say it outright, but... he hinted as much. I think he's found out, Jess. And now, with the pregnancy..."

"What? How could he know about that?" she muttered. Jessica's blood ran cold. The pregnancy. She had confided in Laura about it just days ago, over coffee at the local Costa, explaining how she wasn't sure who the father was. Laura had been her confidante, her rock in a situation that felt impossible to navigate. Her hand covered her mouth, and she shook her head. What a mess. It seemed like her world was on the verge of crumbling.

Lowering her hand, she whispered, "Laura, I... I haven't told him about the baby." Her voice continued to tremble when she added, "I don't even know if it's his."

Laura shuffled towards her and hooked an arm around her shoulder. "You need to be honest with him, Jess. You can't keep this from him for too long. You're already showing."

Jessica nodded slowly. Her gaze dropped to the slight bump, and she placed a protective hand over the tiny human growing inside her. She knew she had to face the inevitable—and tell Daniel. She wouldn't be able to keep the secret much longer, not with the possibility that he already knew. But she feared how he would react to the news—what he might do—to the extent that it paralysed her.

"Oh God, what shall I do? I've got to tell him. Yes, that's what I'll do. I'll tell him tonight," she said, more to herself than to Laura. "I'll have to come clean... for all our sakes."

Laura gave her a reassuring squeeze and sighed. "Good. You'll feel better once it's all out in the open, love. I'll be here if you need me, you know that. Through thick and thin, like always."

Jessica nodded and watched Laura rise to her feet.

"I have to go. I just popped by on the off-chance that you'd be at home. I have a dentist's appointment around the corner."

"Thanks for dropping in and making me aware of the situation. Good luck at the dentist. I had to have a filling the last time I went; it hurt like hell. Sorry, I shouldn't have told you that."

"I'm used to it. I don't mind being tortured by mine. Looking into his gorgeous eyes sends me into oblivion most of the time. He could remove all my teeth during a single visit, and I probably wouldn't notice. I'll call you later, unless you ring me first. The choice is yours."

"I'll see how things go with Daniel and give you a bell later, if I can."

"Okay, I'll wait to hear from you. Be strong, hon. Remember, you have a baby to consider now. The less stress, the better, or so I've heard." Laura pecked her on the cheek and left the house.

Jessica waved her off and stood on the doorstep until Laura slipped into her car, the weight of Laura's words settling on her shoulders. Jessica sensed everything was about to change forever. The perfect life she had, and her meticulously constructed marriage, would be completely disrupted. But there was no other option; it couldn't be avoided, not if Daniel had learnt the truth about her affair.

Her anxiety escalated to another level as the evening descended. She paced the living room, constantly watching the clock, waiting for her husband to come home. Her mind wandered now and again to Paul's text, to the affair she had tried to leave behind. After hours of consideration, she concluded that she had to cut ties with him once and for all. But before she could do what was needed, she had to face Daniel.

She prepared the evening meal and sat down to eat, but instead, she ended up pushing the food around the plate, not feeling hungry in the slightest once the pasta had been cooked. She'd rung him many times, only for his phone to go straight to voicemail. Hours passed, and Daniel still hadn't come home. Jessica checked her phone again—no messages, no missed calls. Her anxiety reached another level, her hands shook and sweat poured from her brow. Where was he? Should she call the police? Report him missing? What if he'd had an accident?

Finally, at five minutes to midnight, she heard the front door creak open. Jessica's heart skipped a beat as Daniel stepped inside and shook the rain from his coat. He glanced at her, his expression unreadable. She suspected he was surprised to see her still up, awaiting his return.

"Where have you been?" Jessica asked, her voice calm despite the anger raging inside her.

Daniel hung his coat on the rack by the door then walked past her into the living room. "Out. I needed some air after work."

Jessica followed him, her nerves on edge, her stomach tied in knots. She dreaded what was to come. This wasn't like Daniel. He was usually so composed, so predictable.

She took the plunge and hesitantly began the conversation she sensed they needed to have. "Daniel, we need to talk," she said, her voice shaking slightly.

With his back to her, he flung the angry words over his shoulder. "About what?"

Jessica closed her eyes and swallowed down the lump lodged in her throat. "About... us. About everything."

Slowly, he faced her, staring at every inch of her face for what seemed like an eternity. Eventually, with his lip curled and his eyes narrowed, he asked, "Is there something you want to tell me, Jess? Something on your mind? Because if there is, now would be a good time."

His disturbing words hung in the air, heavy with accusation. Jessica's heart pounded violently against her ribs. She hated any form of confrontation. There was no doubt in her mind what he was getting at. He knew. She wondered if he had known for longer than she realised. And now, standing there in the silence of their lavish home, she could feel the weight of her secrets pressing down on her.

"Daniel, I..." She hesitated, the words catching in her throat, making her want to claw at her delicate skin to release them. How could she tell him about the affair, about the baby, about everything she had kept hidden for the past few months?

But before she could say anything, Daniel's phone buzzed in his pocket. He glanced at it, his face tightening as he read the message.

"This will have to wait. I'm needed elsewhere. I have to go," he snapped. He grabbed his coat and slipped it on, then turned towards the door.

Stunned, she shouted, "Wait, what? Now? You can't. We have things we need to discuss. It's late. What on earth could be so important?"

"It's a work thing," Daniel muttered and reached for the door handle.

Jessica watched as he hurried out of the door and got into his BMW, leaving her standing alone, her confession sitting on the tip of her tongue.

She closed the door, her mind spinning. Something was very wrong. She wondered what else was going on, sensing that the affair was nothing in comparison, or was that her imagination working overtime?

Jessica poured herself a brandy nightcap and promptly threw it down the sink. *I can't, not now that I'm pregnant. I desperately want this child, but at what cost?* Even though it was late, getting close to twelve-thirty, she ran herself a bath to soak away the emotions churning inside. Feeling more relaxed, she admired her profile in the mirrored wardrobe and considered what it would be like to have a baby to hold. Something she'd never contemplated before. She'd been married to Daniel for seven years now; both of them were worka-holics. The subject of starting a family one day had never come up during their marriage. Now that the reality had struck, she was grad-ually getting used to the idea, even though it scared her shitless.

She slipped into bed and, still wide awake, picked up her book and opened it. She soon became engrossed in the thriller, any thoughts of Daniel walking out on her forgotten, until her phone tinkled, indicating that a message had arrived. It was from Paul.

Meet me tomorrow. We need to settle this.

Jessica closed her eyes, feeling the walls of her life closing in around her. Tomorrow. Tomorrow, everything would change. Tomor-row, she would have to face the consequences of her choices.

1

The bitterly cold Hereford morning greeted Detective Inspector Sara Ramsey as she left the house earlier than usual. Another sleepless night meant she had fallen out with her husband, Mark. Guilt accompanied her on the drive to work. It wasn't his fault. He was under pressure, as well. With the lack of vets in Hereford at present, the onus was on him to put in the extra hours needed to care for all the ill or injured animals north of the river. His recent health scare was a constant worry to both of them. He wouldn't get the all-clear from cancer, not yet, despite the consultant reassuring them that all signs of it had been eradicated with the removal of his testicle. She parked up in her allocated space and made a run for it. The drizzle, the kind that soaked through your coat before you even realised it, soured her mood. The wind suddenly got up, and she battled with the door to the main entrance of the police station. "Bloody hell, it's getting worse out there."

The desk sergeant, Jeff Makepeace, stifled a yawn and apologised. "Sorry, ma'am."

Sara approached the counter and asked, "Everything all right, Jeff? You look shattered."

"Short-staffed. I've been on duty since four this morning." He lowered his voice to add, "I'm getting too old for this crap."

"It's getting beyond a joke. You shouldn't be expected to cover someone else's shift as well as your own. Do you want me to have a word with the chief?"

"Extenuating circumstances. There are so many people off sick with some illness or other. Personally, I haven't had a day off sick in twenty years of service."

"They broke the mould when you were born, Jeff. I don't think I've had a sickie in over five years. I haven't had the time." Sara smiled. "Any news since you came on duty?"

"As it happens, yes. I've just handed the file to Carla; she's only been in five minutes or so."

Sara shook her head. "She's in? I'm so used to being the first to arrive, I didn't even check if anyone else's car was here. Is she all right?"

He shrugged. "She appears to be. I think her motor is in the garage today, so she got a lift in with Des."

"Ah, that would explain it. Okay, I won't hold you up any longer. Make sure you get plenty of caffeine inside you to help see you through your shift."

"I will. I've already had six cups, to my knowledge. Not something I'd admit to the wife, of course."

She entered her passcode into the keypad, and the door sprang open. Sara said good morning to a couple of uniformed officers as she passed them on the stairs. Reaching the incident room, she glanced through the glass panel in the door to see Carla scratching her head while she flicked through the papers in a manila folder.

Sara burst into the room and shouted, "Morning!"

Carla stared at her and slammed a hand to her chest. "What the fu... you scared the shit out of me."

Sara laughed. "Sorry, I couldn't resist it. You were so engrossed in your work."

"I'll get you for that before the day is out."

"I'm genuinely sorry. Jeff mentioned that he'd given you a case to read. Want to tell me what it's all about over a cup of coffee?"

"Why not? My first cup has gone cold. How come you're in so early?"

"I couldn't sleep, and Mark and I were getting on each other's nerves, so I thought I'd make an early start to keep the peace. Jeff told me your car is in the garage. Nothing serious, I hope?"

"A slight knocking in the engine. I thought I'd told you. I booked it in at the end of last week. Sod this, coming in to work at the crack of dawn."

"Crack of dawn?"

"Well, seven-thirty, that's too damn early for me."

Sara sniggered. "You're a scream." She crossed the room to the drinks station and poured them both a coffee, then returned to see what was causing her partner to scratch her head so much. "What have we got?" She pulled a chair up to sit alongside Carla.

"Do you want to read the file yourself, or would you prefer that I give you a quick rundown?"

"The latter," Sara said and sipped on her coffee.

"Only if you promise to hear me out first."

"Of course. That sounds ominous. Fire away, when you're ready."

Carla fidgeted in her chair and cleared her throat. "I know it's not something we generally deal with, not this soon, but Jeff and I are of the same opinion..."

Sara sighed and gestured with her hand for Carla to hurry up and get to the point.

"All right, you impatient so-and-so. The station received a call at around four-fifteen this morning from Daniel Harding."

Sara frowned and searched her memory. "I recognise the name, but that's as far as it goes. Who is he?"

"He's a local investment banker. But this is where you're probably more familiar with him. He's married to one of the top solicitors in the area, Jessica Harding."

"Yes, that's right. How could I forget? Why did he contact the station at that time of the morning?"

"To report his wife missing."

Sara sat upright and swivelled the file to face her. "What? Let me read that."

Carla snorted and sat back. "Be my guest."

It took her a few minutes to read the details of the call Daniel had made in the early hours of the morning. "Missing, one of Hereford's top lawyers. Vanished from her exclusive home. No signs of forced entry from what the husband could see and no sign of a struggle either."

"And no ransom demand, not as yet," Carla added.

Sara ran through the particulars one more time and then pushed the file across the desk to her partner. "I'm with you. Something isn't adding up." A gnawing instinct in her gut had instantly appeared as soon as she realised that Jessica was involved. She inhaled a calming breath and rubbed at her makeup-free eyes. She had a feeling this case was going to be far from easy. "Have you started the background checks on both of them?"

"I've made a start, in between reading the file. They bought the house, a new build out at Stretton Sugwas, two years ago. It's part of an exclusive estate that was designed and built by exceptional builders from Worcester. I found an article in the local paper. Here's a picture of the happy couple standing outside the magnificent house." Carla angled the screen Sara's way.

"You're right, they seem exceptionally happy, but then, so would I be with a house like that. Wouldn't you?"

Carla fiddled with her ponytail, pulling it tighter as she nodded. "Yep, what's not to love about that place? Although something that size would be too bloody large for me and Des."

"Yeah, you're not wrong. Mark and I would spend most of our spare time playing 'hunt our partners' in a house that large. I'm guessing they don't have any kids to share it with?"

"Not yet. According to the article, they're both workaholics and haven't got the time to start a family."

"Blimey, I bet they rattle around in it." Sara frowned and reread a section of the notes that she found puzzling. "Hang on, it says here that he reported her missing at four-fifteen, but the last time he saw her was at around eight last night. Why did he wait eight hours before he reported her missing? It seems a long time for a worried husband to wait before calling the police."

Carla sat back and folded her arms. "My sentiments exactly. When Jeff asked him what was behind the delay, Harding told him they hadn't seen eye to eye over something and spent the evening apart. I suppose, looking at the size of their house, that's not inconceivable. According to Daniel, Jessica went upstairs to the bedroom. He stayed downstairs, watching a film in the cinema room. Later, he fell asleep in one of the comfy chairs and woke up at around two. When he went up to bed, she was missing. He didn't think anything of it at the time, assumed she might have gone out for a drive, which she often did to clear her head."

"At that time of the morning? What about her car? Is that missing too?" Sara clawed the file back. "Nope, it was sitting in the garage all along. When asked if anything else was missing, he told Jeff that nothing appeared to be and there was no sign of forced entry. He swore blind that he locked the front door when they got home earlier that evening."

Sara adjusted her position to look at the computer screen, her brow furrowed as she studied Jessica Harding's photo: mid-thirties, dark hair, confident smile. A woman with everything going for her— a successful career, a well-off husband, and a seemingly perfect life. Sara had seen these types of pictures a hundred times before. The smile for the camera often held grave secrets. She couldn't help wondering if that was the case this time.

"And the husband? Daniel Harding?" Sara asked. "What do we know about him?"

"He's an investment banker. Seems genuine enough, but something about his story feels off to me. He told Jeff they've been happily married for seven years with no major issues, just the usual marital bumps in the road here and there. That picture looks so false. He's hiding something. You can see it in his eyes." Carla's voice dropped slightly. "I'd bet six months' salary there's more to this than he's letting on."

Sara nodded, taking in the information. She trusted Carla's instincts—her partner had a knack for sniffing out inconsistencies, and Sara had learned to listen when Carla suspected something was brewing. Still, they would need more than gut instincts before they started throwing any accusations around.

"I know you haven't been working on this for long, but what about her friends? Family? Anyone we should talk to?" Sara asked.

"I got on that straight away. Thought you would want to hit the ground running as soon as you were aware of the details. I've already lined up a few interviews. Her best friend, Laura Whitfield, seems like a good place to start. She was one of the last people to see Jessica before she went missing. I've got her coming in later today for a chat. I'm also doing the usual research into Jessica's colleagues at her law firm."

Sara glanced at the clock on the wall. It was just after eight-fifteen, and already the day felt long. "Excellent, you've done well, considering how long you've been at it. Let's get out there and talk to the husband." She grabbed her coat off the back of her chair. "See if we can shake things up a bit. If he's hiding something, we'll soon find out."

Carla stood, her energy matching Sara's as they raced out of the incident room and down the stairs to the reception area.

Sara flung her car keys at Carla. "I won't be long. I need to have a chat with Jeff before we leave."

Her partner nodded and exited the main door.

"Jeff, we're heading out to interview Daniel Harding. Can you do me a favour and let the rest of my team know when they arrive?"

"Consider it done, and good luck, ma'am. I hope you get some useful information out of him."

"I think we've all got our suspicions about him. I'm going to need to keep mine in check during the interview." She gave him a knowing wink and followed Carla out to the car.

Carla waited until Sara started the engine and had pulled out of the car park, then she asked, "You think he's behind it?"

Sara contemplated the question for a moment. "Hard to say without meeting him. Nevertheless, statistics indicate that in the majority of cases where a wife goes missing, the husband is implicated. He might—I did say *might*—be the exception to the rule. What's the address? Can you punch it in for me?"

"Sorry, I should have done that while I was waiting for you."

Sara grinned. "You can make up for your mistake now."

By the time they reached Stretton Sugwas, the dark grey clouds had dispersed, and it had thankfully stopped raining. The impressive estate of classy individual homes took Sara's breath away. "And I thought I had a decent new build. These are mega nice, taking it to the extreme. Would I want to live here? I doubt it. While they seem impressive, on the flip side, they're not enticing me to rush out and rob a bank to buy one."

"What the fu... are you for real?" Carla chuckled beside her.

"Shit! Did I say that out loud? Sorry, my fault. Come on, I'm eager to see what luxury awaits us on the inside."

Sara rang the bell. The door was immediately answered by a tall man in his mid-thirties. His hair was neatly combed, but his blood-shot eyes told Sara that he'd been up most of the night. However, he was still dressed to impress in a grey pinstriped suit. His expression oozed composure, which for some reason put Sara on edge.

She flashed her warrant card. "Mr Harding? I'm DI Sara Ramsey, and this is my partner, DS Carla Jameson. Is it convenient to have a chat with you about your wife?"

He glanced at his watch. "I have to leave for work in twenty minutes. Will that be long enough, Inspector?"

You've just reported your wife missing and here you are, considering going to work? That seems a tad off to me. Daniel stepped behind the door and gestured for them to enter the pristine hallway. There was nothing out of place in the vast area. It was far too sterile for Sara's liking. She resisted the urge to shudder as she studied her surroundings, quickly coming to the conclusion that it lacked any warmth. If anything, the hallway left her feeling cold in an eerie sort of way.

"Thank you for coming out to see me so promptly. I know you rarely entertain a missing person case until twenty-four hours have passed. Or is that just a myth these days?" his voice was low and measured. "I'll do whatever I can to help you find my dear wife."

Sara and Carla entered the house. "It is. Shall we take our shoes off?"

"No, it's fine. We have a cleaner who comes in three times a week. She's due today at around eleven. Shall we go through to the lounge?"

Sara smiled, then she and Carla followed him across the hallway into the huge lounge. Three of the walls were made of glass, showing off the magnificent view of the garden. A swimming pool dominated the patio area, and beyond, the lawn and borders were immaculately presented, obviously tended by a professional rather than an enthusiastic gardener.

"We understand you reported your wife missing this morning. Would you mind going over the details with us?"

"Of course. Please, take a seat." His jaw tightened. He glanced at the rug under the glass table between the two sofas and sighed. "Let me see now. We had dinner at around seven. Do you need to know what we ate?"

"No, that's fine. Please continue."

"Everything seemed fine between us. During our meal we discussed how our day had panned out at work. Afterwards we tidied up and loaded the dishwasher. Then we had a... discussion. No, it was more of a disagreement about something minor. She didn't like my response and stormed off to the bedroom."

"Can you tell us what the disagreement was about?"

He ran a hand around his face, then clenched his hands together and rested his forearms on his thighs. "I'm trying to think; it must have been something insignificant. Otherwise, I would remember, right?"

Sara smiled, but his demeanour made her more suspicious. "So, Jessica went upstairs, and what did you do?"

"I watched *Maverick* in the cinema room. I must have dropped off during the credits at the end. When I woke up, it was two in the morning. I went up to bed and crept around the bedroom, not wanting to wake her. It wasn't until I got into bed and found it empty that I began to worry. At first, I thought she'd gone out for some fresh air. She does that quite often at night because she suffers from migraines. When she didn't come back by four, it suddenly dawned on me to check the garage. Her car was still inside. It was a toss-up between getting in the car and searching the immediate area for her or calling the police. I decided on the latter. You're not going to hold that against me, are you?"

"So, you left it another fifteen minutes before you rang us, is that correct?" Sara challenged, her eyebrows raised.

"I searched every room in the house—there are quite a few, as you can imagine," he said, a note of sarcasm creeping into his tone. "Then I fetched a torch and went outside. Sometimes, when she's trying to get rid of a migraine, she'll do a couple of circuits of the garden."

"I should think that would be dependent on the weather. What was it like at that time of the morning?"

He glared at her and ground his teeth. "I believe it had just started raining again. It had been on and off all night."

"Does Jessica often walk around the garden in the rain?"

His gaze intensified, and he chewed on his bottom lip. "Sometimes, it depends on the severity of the migraine," he responded, without having to think the answer through first. "Look, I thought she would come back. We're a married couple. Arguments are part and parcel of married bliss, aren't they? Are you married, Inspector?" He peered at her ring finger to check.

"I am. My husband and I rarely argue, sir. But every marriage is different."

"Ain't that the truth?" he grumbled. "I'm getting the impression that you're blaming me for not searching thoroughly for her. Wouldn't you have covered all the angles first before reporting your husband missing? There was no reason for her to go. She hasn't taken her car. She'd never go anywhere without it."

"Only to walk off a migraine," Sara added and scrutinised his reaction.

"It's never easy to know what to do in these circumstances. I'd hate to be accused of overreacting."

"Indeed. What about her family and friends? Have you checked if anyone has seen her during the night?"

"No, I haven't got around to doing that. I have a very important meeting I need to attend, and I'm in the habit of leaving it until the last minute to make any notes needed. That's what I've been doing since I logged her missing."

I'm not sure I'd be able to concentrate on work if Mark went missing; in fact, I know I wouldn't be able to. Sara continued to monitor his reactions, her previous suspicions still lingering. Nothing he'd told them so far had given her any reason to believe that what he was saying was the truth. There was something dodgy about his behaviour. His reactions and responses almost seemed rehearsed. *Maybe I'm doing him an injustice; maybe not. I've met his type a few times over the years. His story had a ring of truth; however, the edges were too neat and too calculated.* She decided to press a little harder. "Mr Harding, is there anything else you haven't told us? Any reason someone might want to harm your wife?"

His eyes darkened, and his fists clenched as he dropped his arms down by his sides. "Not that I know of," he replied firmly. "My wife is a good woman. As far as I know, she hasn't made any enemies over the years. If something has happened to her, I doubt if it's because of anything she's knowingly done."

Sara exchanged a glance with Carla. There it was—that note of defensiveness, the refusal to consider any possibility that didn't align with his carefully constructed narrative. They definitely needed to dig deeper.

"We'll leave it there for now. Thank you for your time, Mr Harding." Sara rose from her seat, and Carla did the same. Her partner tucked her notebook into her jacket pocket. "We'll be in touch. In the meantime, if you think of anything else—anything at all—please let us know."

Daniel gave an abrupt nod and showed them through the hallway to the front door. He didn't offer his hand, and neither did Sara. "I'll be sure to let you know."

Sara handed him a business card, which he accepted and tucked into the pocket of his waistcoat.

During their walk back to the car, Carla let out a low whistle. "Well, he's obviously hiding something."

Sara nodded in agreement and pressed the key fob to unlock the doors. "We'll see what his wife's friends have to say. Maybe we'll get a clearer picture once we've spoken to them."

As she drove out of the driveway, Sara's mind raced with dozens of questions. Something felt very off about this case. The Hardings weren't just any ordinary couple, and Jessica Harding's disappearance was more than just a random event. But the truth, whatever it was, was still buried deep beneath layers of secrets.

And Sara was determined to get to the bottom of it. No matter whose toes she stood on along the way.

2

On the way to the station, Sara considered moving the interview location for Laura Whitfield. By doing so, she hoped the woman would become more open with them, rather than in the restricted setting of an interview room at the police station.

"Hello, Laura? This is DI Sara Ramsey. Is it convenient to talk?" Sara hit the speaker on her phone.

"Oh, hi. Yes, I was just on my way to the station to meet you. Is there something wrong?"

"No, there's nothing wrong, apart from the obvious. Would it be all right with you if we changed the location of our meeting? We quite often use a café in town, in the alley close to Tesco. Do you know it?"

"I think so. It's in a courtyard. Is that the one? Actually, that suits me better. I'll set off now. It should only take me five, maybe ten minutes at the most, to get there."

"Fabulous. I look forward to seeing you soon." Sara ended the call and indicated left at the roundabout. The slip road took them underground to the supermarket car park. Sara flicked open her secret compartment and withdrew one pound fifty. "Will you get the ticket?"

Carla held out her hand for the coins. Her partner returned moments later, and they headed towards the café. Inside, Sara pointed at the table by the window, and Carla took a seat while she placed the orders. "Just a coffee?"

"Please. Flat white, if they have one," Carla confirmed.

Sara smiled at the middle-aged woman serving. "Two flat white coffees, thanks. We're expecting someone else to join us. Can you leave the bill open, or would you rather I pay now?"

"I can leave it open for you, no problem. Not tempted to have a slice of one of our homemade cakes?"

"We shouldn't. We're supposed to be working. We've sampled them before, and they're delicious. I recommend your café all the time."

"Thank you. I recognise your face. Do you work in one of the offices nearby?"

Sara leaned closer and whispered, "Try the police station. My partner and I are detectives."

The woman's mouth dropped open. She recovered quickly and said, "Wow, that's amazing. I don't think I've met a plainclothes officer before. We're honoured that you've chosen to visit us."

"Thanks. Your food is too tempting to ignore."

The bell sounded behind Sara. She turned to see a young, tall, elegant woman closing the door.

Sara took a punt and asked, "Are you Laura?"

"Hi, yes. Are you Inspector Raymond?"

"It's Ramsey. You can call me Sara. What would you like to drink?"

"I can get my own."

"Don't worry, I'll get it on expenses."

Laura smiled and glanced over her shoulder. "I'll have an Americano then, thanks. I haven't been here before. I've passed it on my way home but never dropped in."

"We come here quite often, but don't tell my boss." Sara pointed at the table where Carla was sitting. "Take a seat with my partner. I believe you spoke with her first thing."

"I will, thanks."

Sara settled up with the woman behind the counter and asked for a receipt.

"I'll bring your drinks over in a moment."

"Great."

Sara joined Carla and Laura. "Thanks for agreeing to meet us here. Sometimes, the station interview rooms can be a bit stuffy and off-putting if you're not used to them."

"I appreciate the change of location. Do you have any news about Jessica?"

"Sadly not. We know what a difficult time this must be for all her friends and family. Talking to more people will hopefully assist us in connecting the dots and get to the bottom of what has really happened to Jessica."

It was hard to tell which side of the coin Laura was going to come down on after their initial introduction. Although Carla had told her that Laura's tone had been clipped when the interview was arranged, Sara made excuses for the young woman's mood, considering Carla had spoken to her at around seven a.m.

"When was the last time you saw her?" Sara asked.

Laura's stern expression slipped away, and her eyes darted between Sara and Carla. "This is all just... so horrible. I can't believe Jessica is missing."

"I know the news must have come as a shock," Sara said calmly, offering a reassuring nod. "Can you tell me when you last saw Jessica?" she repeated.

The waitress delivered their coffees, pausing their conversation.

Laura reached for two sachets of brown sugar, tipped them into her coffee, and then stirred it. "Yesterday evening. I called at her house after work. I think it was at around six or thereabouts. She seemed a little agitated. Maybe that's the wrong word. Perhaps *stressed* would be more accurate, but nothing out of the ordinary. She has a stressful career and has been known to take her work home with her, if you get what I mean."

"She found it hard to switch off at the end of the day?" Sara asked.

"Yes, that's it."

"What did you talk about?" Sara took a sip of her coffee, her gaze never leaving Laura.

Laura swallowed and twisted her cup in the saucer. The noise grated on Sara's nerves.

"We talked about... well, personal things. I didn't think much of it at the time," Laura added dismissively.

"Personal things?" Carla interjected, her eyes narrowing. "Could you elaborate for us?"

Laura hesitated, her fingers tightening around the rim of the cup. "Jessica has been... going through some stuff lately. I was there to lend an ear and to possibly give her some answers to a dilemma that has been troubling her. She wasn't sure what to do about it. She confided in me and vice versa. It was my turn to offer her my shoulder to cry on. But I don't know if it's relevant to her going missing."

"In order for us to investigate her disappearance, you're going to have to tell us what kind of personal matters you're alluding to," Sara pressed, her tone firm but gentle, already sensing that they weren't getting anywhere fast.

Laura glanced around the café as if searching for an escape, then lowered her voice. "Jessica told me that she was pregnant."

Sara inclined her head. "Oh, I see. Did Daniel know?"

Laura shook her head. "No, she was trying to pluck up the courage to tell him. And... there's more." She continued to twist her cup in the saucer.

"What's that?" Sara probed, different scenarios tearing through her mind.

Laura cleared her throat. Her voice came out raspy and raw. "There was someone else involved. Another man."

Sara's gaze flicked towards Carla for the briefest of moments. This was the kind of information they'd been hoping to uncover. "Another man?" she asked, her tone neutral. "Who?"

Laura's mouth opened and closed a few times before she finally gave them a name. "His name is Paul Grant," she whispered and scanned the area to check that no one had overheard her. After a few seconds of silence, she added, "He's a solicitor at the same firm as Jessica."

"I see. So, an office affair. How long has it been going on, do you know?" Sara asked.

"A few months, I believe. She told me it was over. She told me she wasn't sure who the father is, and that's what was freaking her out. I believe she was scared of how Daniel would react."

"Were they intending to have kids, eventually?"

"No, I don't think so. They're both dedicated to their careers. I don't think either of them was fussed about having children."

"What about Paul? Did he know? Did Jessica mention anything about his reaction to the pregnancy?" Carla chipped in when Sara paused too long between questions.

Laura shook her head. "No, as far as I know, she hasn't told him. She was planning to end things with him for good, with the intention of focusing on her marriage. Her heart truly belongs to Daniel. She loves him, despite everything, and she's desperate to put things right between them."

Sara nodded, processing the information. "As she confided in you, did she say if she was worried about anyone else? Anyone she was associated with, either personally or professionally, who might want to hurt her?"

"I can't recall her ever mentioning that she was *scared* of anyone. Jessica is normally in full control of her life. Does that seem an odd thing to say? It's really the only way I can describe her."

"No, it's fine. It gives us a good insight into what type of person she is."

"But saying that, she has seemed... different recently. Maybe a tad anxious, as if she were afraid of something, but she wouldn't tell me what."

"Might that have been because of the pregnancy?"

Laura shrugged and then took a sip of her coffee. "Possibly. It's hard to know what to think when your best friend puts the shutters up on you like that."

"But she didn't. If that were the case, she wouldn't have told you about the pregnancy, would she?"

Sighing, Laura nodded. "I suppose that's true. Sorry, I'm not trying to make excuses, but my mind has been working overtime, thinking up all sorts of crap since Carla rang me this morning. I tried to call Daniel as soon as I found out, but his phone was switched off. I thought that was strange. I mean, what if Jessica had tried to get in touch with him?"

"I agree with you, that is strange. We didn't bother calling him, we just showed up at the house. He was dressed, ready for an important meeting."

"What the...? How can he even consider going to work at a time like this—when Jess is missing? That's disgusting. He should be ashamed of himself."

Sara raised a hand. "In our experience, people react in different ways when a loved one goes missing. Don't worry, we'll keep a close eye on him."

"Good."

"What else can you tell us about the other man, Paul, wasn't it?"

"Umm... he's good-looking. Single, which came as a shock to me. Or, as Jess put it, 'he's between girlfriends'. He's relatively new at the office, started working there less than six months ago, something like that."

Sara exchanged a look with Carla. They'd just been handed their first actual suspect, and the picture of Jessica Harding's life was growing more complicated by the minute.

"Thank you, Laura," Sara said. "This helps us a lot. We'll be in touch if we need anything else."

Laura nodded, her eyes brimming with unshed tears. "Please, just find her. She's my best friend. She's out there somewhere, in need of our help."

"Don't worry, we'll find her, unless she doesn't want to be found."

Laura gasped. "What are you saying? That she might have run off intentionally?"

"We can't rule it out, although Daniel informed us that Jess's car was still in the garage."

"There you are then. Jess never goes anywhere without her pride and joy. She bought it at the end of last year with a substantial bonus she received from the firm."

"Very nice. Is she a partner there?"

"No, they asked her—or should I say, pleaded with her—to become a partner, but she didn't want the added responsibility. She's happy as she is. I think she's on a decent salary, not that she's ever revealed what that is. There are some things in this life you should keep from your best friends, salary being one of them."

"I understand. Okay, if there's nothing else you can tell us, then we'll wrap things up here, if that's okay?"

"No, nothing that I can think of. Perhaps if you give me a card, I can give you a call if anything comes to mind."

Sara smiled, removed a card from her pocket and slid it across the table. "I was about to suggest the same."

They all downed the last of their drinks and left the café together.

At the end of the courtyard, Sara said, "Thanks again for meeting with us and giving us an insight into Jessica's personality and what is going on in her life at the moment."

"My pleasure. I hope it helps you find her. Bye for now. Give me a call if you need to ask any further questions."

"Ditto. Try not to worry about your friend too much."

"I'll try." Laura waved and trotted off towards the town centre.

Sara and Carla headed in the opposite direction, back to the car.

"What did you make of her?" Carla asked.

"She seemed nice enough. The information she gave us could be vital to the investigation. It didn't take her long to tell us about the affair and the unexpected, or should I say, unwanted, pregnancy. Sounds like plenty of motive for someone to get rid of her, don't you think?"

"I was thinking along the same lines. The plot thickens," Carla agreed.

Sara paused and withdrew her phone from her pocket. "Let's see what the firm says about him." She brought up the Richards and Grant website and checked out the information for each of the solicitors listed. "Hmm... Paul Grant, despite only being at the firm for six months, he's a senior partner there. Well-respected, but there's always more lying beneath the surface. We know that from our vast experience. Laura was right about one thing."

Carla frowned and asked, "What was that?"

"He's gobsmackingly handsome."

"Sorry to correct you, but I believe the term she used was *good-looking*."

Sara chuckled. "Trust me to embellish the truth."

During their journey back to the car they bounced ideas around between them.

"If he found out about the pregnancy and it wasn't his... that could push a man to do something desperate," Carla suggested.

"Who are you talking about? Daniel or Paul?"

Carla shrugged and puffed out her cheeks. "Exactly. Take your pick. It could be either one of them."

"Possibly. Or Paul might have been using her to climb his way up the ladder, and once he'd achieved the partnership, maybe she threatened to end it, which made him snap."

"What are you going to do next?"

"I'll take the official route, ring the station and ask Jill to give him a call, invite him in for questioning."

"To drive home that you mean business from the get-go?"

Sara grinned at her partner. "You're learning. Hey, and congratulations on jumping in and asking questions back there. You need to do that more often."

"I've never been one for stepping on your toes, Sara."

"No, I mean it. I'm giving you permission to do it from now on. We're partners. We should both be capable of asking what's on our mind during an interview."

"It's hard sometimes, especially if I'm the one taking the notes."

"I'll let you off that one. Let me give Jill a call before we go underground, in case it affects my phone service." Sara rang the station. "Jill, it's me. Sorry Carla and I weren't there to greet you and the rest of the team first thing. I hope Jeff brought you up to date with what's going on?"

"He did, boss. We've been busy carrying out the background checks. No chance of any camera footage in the area, not unless the Harding residence has got security cameras."

"Hmm... I didn't think to ask when we visited the husband. Remiss of me, I know. I'll contact him later. Can you do me a favour and give Paul Grant at Richards and Grant Solicitors a call?"

"I can, boss. What do you need from him?"

"I need him to come in for questioning ASAP. We've uncovered an interesting fact, that Paul Grant and Jessica Harding were having an affair."

"Ouch, I see. I'm on it now."

"I know we'd usually drop by and see him at his place of work, but I want to handle this case differently because of the information we've gathered so far."

"Understandable. I'll make the call and get back to you soon."

Sara paced the area at the top of the slip road that led to the car park until Jill got back to her.

"It's me," Jill said. "He's on his way in. He told me it's the only spare time he's got today."

"Did he ask what the meeting was about?" Sara asked.

"No, and I didn't hint at anything either."

"Excellent. We're on the edge of town. We shouldn't be long." Sara ended the call and headed back to the car, the weight of Laura's revelation hanging over her.

By the time they arrived at the station, Paul Grant was already in one of the interview rooms waiting for them.

Sara stopped off at the reception area and asked the desk sergeant, "How did he seem to you?"

"Fine. Not fazed by having to come in at all."

"Okay, that's interesting. Thanks, Jeff. Can you arrange for some drinks to be brought in, please?"

"They're on their way. He's already put his order in."

Sara smiled and punched her code into the security keypad. The door clicked open. She and Carla walked the length of the grey corridor to Interview Room One at the end.

Paul Grant was standing when they entered the room. A tall man in his early forties, who appeared to be composed in his strange surroundings. Sara recognised him from some of the cases they'd worked on that had gone to court recently, also from the company's website. Although he hadn't been the lead prosecutor, he'd sat alongside some of them as part of the legal team. She also picked up that there was something guarded about his posture.

Sara introduced herself and Carla, then invited him to take a seat opposite them. He immediately clasped his hands in front of him, and his gaze drifted between them. She sensed they were in for a rough ride. There was also a tension in his jaw that caught Sara's attention.

"I'd like to thank you for coming in at such short notice, Mr Grant."

"My pleasure. You can call me Paul. Is this to do with a case I've been working on, Inspector? Only your colleague was very vague on the phone when she asked me to come in."

"Not exactly. Paul, we understand that you work closely with Jessica Harding. Is that correct?"

His brow furrowed. "Yes, she works alongside me. May I ask why you want to know?"

"I'm not sure if you're aware, but Jessica was reported missing this morning by her husband. We'd like to ask you a few questions about her disappearance, if that's okay?"

"What? I didn't know. I knew she was absent from work this morning, but I assumed she had an out-of-office appointment with a client. It's not unheard of in our line of business. We try to accommodate our clients as much as possible." He ran a hand through his short hair, then smoothed it in place again. "I'm shocked to hear this. How can I help?"

"We've spoken with someone who knows Jessica really well, and your name came up during our enquiries."

"Hardly surprising, considering we work together. Who did you speak to?"

"One of Jessica's good friends."

"I bet I can guess who that is," he mumbled.

Sara spotted a chink in his composure, and he wrung his hands together. "It has come to our attention that you and Jessica were more than just colleagues. Is that true?"

A flicker of surprise crossed his face. He stretched out his neck and twisted his head to the left and then to the right. "That's correct. Jessica and I... were involved. We knew it couldn't go anywhere."

"Are you telling me the affair was over?"

"Yes, we discussed it a few weeks ago, and it was Jessica who decided to end it. She told me she wanted to focus on her heavy case-load and to repair what had gone wrong in her marriage. We're both adults. I respected her decision."

"And what about the pregnancy?" Carla jumped in to ask.

His head jutted forward, and his jaw dropped open. Regaining his composure, he shook his head and asked quietly, "Pregnancy? I didn't know."

"She didn't tell you?" Sara pressed, unconvinced.

He shook his head several times. Sweat appeared on his top lip, and he wiped it away with his hand. "Good Lord, no, I didn't know. This is the first I've heard about it. Hang on, I know how these things work. I hope you're not suggesting I had anything to do with her disappearance. Are you? I care about her. She wasn't a quick fling to me. There's no way on this earth that I'd want to hurt her. Jesus... pregnant."

Sara studied him for a long moment, weighing his words. He seemed genuinely caught off-guard by the mention of the pregnancy, but that didn't clear him of suspicion, not in her opinion. There was something in his reaction that was telling her he couldn't be trusted. Intent on keeping the pressure on him, she asked, "And how would you have responded if she'd told you?"

He heaved out a breath and ran his hand through his hair again. "You tell me. It's not the type of news I'm used to hearing. I can assure you that no one is more shocked than I am. A baby! Holy shit!"

"Was there talk of Jessica leaving Daniel?"

"No. Didn't you hear me? We slept together—if you can call a quick shag over the desk after hours 'sleeping together'—three, maybe four times. I can't honestly remember."

"Because it meant more to her than to you. Am I right?"

"I don't know. I'm single; she's the one who is married. My conscience is clear, it always has been."

Sara's eyes narrowed. She didn't like this man. She'd come across his type many times over the years. His main purpose in life was to use women and discard them when the going got tough. Was that what happened here? "Are you sure you weren't aware of the pregnancy?"

He slammed his fist on the desk, startling Sara and Carla. "I'm sure. Don't you dare lay this at my door, Inspector."

"I sense a threat lingering in that statement, Paul. Is there one?"

"No. All I'm trying to tell you is that I had nothing to do with her going missing. Why won't you believe me?"

"And all I'm doing here is asking pertinent questions about Jessica's relationship with you. Surely you can understand our need to interview someone who has admitted to having an affair with a married woman, can't you? A woman who has since been reported missing by her husband."

He leaned his head back and closed his eyes. "Give me bloody strength." His head lowered again, and he glared at Sara. "All right, I can see how this looks and that you need to investigate what you've been told. But you're going to have to take my word when I tell you I didn't know that she was pregnant. If your next question is going to be a repeat of how I would have reacted to the news... I'm telling you honestly that I don't know. The thought has never occurred to me."

"Did you use condoms during sexual intercourse with Jessica?"

His hand covered his face, and his cheeks flared. He dropped his hand and admitted, "No. It was a spur-of-the-moment thing for both of us. I assumed, what with her being married, that she was on the pill. I'm realising now that probably wasn't the case and I feel foolish for not asking her at the time. I'm sure you can imagine what it's like, when two people are obsessed with each other and just want to rip each other's clothes off."

"It's not something that has ever happened to me, so no, I can't imagine what it must be like, Paul. For your information, condoms also protect people against sexually transmitted diseases."

He stared at her for a while until a grin emerged. "I know what they're for, Inspector. And on the other point I raised, you can't tell me you haven't caught some of your colleagues up to no good in the office after hours over the years."

Sara raised an eyebrow. "Sorry, my colleagues and I are far too professional to allow that to happen."

He growled and shook his head. "That's crap, and you know it."

Sara shrugged. "There's not a lot I can do if you refuse to believe me. Anyway, getting back to why I invited you in for questioning. Can you think of anyone who would want to hurt Jessica?"

His shoulders slumped, and his gaze dropped to his clenched hands, the fight knocked out of him by Sara's put-down. "No, apart from that husband of hers. When did she go missing and in what circumstances?"

"While she was at home last night. Daniel was downstairs, asleep on the couch."

He raised his hands. "There you are then. Job done. The husband is the guilty party. No one else should come under scrutiny."

"It doesn't work like that, Paul. Okay, we can wrap things up now. We'll be in touch with you if we need to ask any further questions. Oh, one last question: where were you last night?"

"At home, working. If I had my laptop with me, I could show you the files I created," he said and rose from his seat.

Sara and Carla accompanied him to the reception area. Sara offered her hand for him to shake, but he chose to ignore it.

"I'm telling you this, Inspector. You're barking up the wrong tree if you think Jess's disappearance is down to me."

"We'll have to see where our enquiries lead us, won't we, Paul? Thanks again for taking the time to stop by and speak with us."

He grunted and left the station. The unease in his posture remained as he walked through the main exit.

Sara turned to Carla and said, "He's hiding something." She crossed her arms and added, "I don't buy the innocent act."

"Agreed," Carla replied. "But we're going to need more."

They made their way back up the stairs.

"I think I'm going to give Daniel a call and ask him to come in for further questioning. He'll need to give us a formal statement, anyway. I can use that as an excuse to get him in here. Also, remind me when he comes in to ask if he has security cameras at the house."

"I will, if I remember," Carla replied with a cheesy grin.

3

An hour later, Sara received a call from Jeff, telling her that Daniel Harding and his solicitor had arrived. She finished off her coffee and set aside the post she was halfway through. "I'm glad to get a break from this crap, and I haven't even touched my emails yet," she grumbled and rose from her seat to collect her partner. "Carla, when you're ready, in other words, now. Harding and his brief have arrived."

They entered the interview room, and Daniel and his solicitor turned to face them.

"Hello, Daniel. Thanks for coming in to see us. Hopefully, we won't keep you too long."

"I hope that's the case, Inspector. This is my solicitor, Warren Townsend."

Sara and Carla took their seats opposite the smartly dressed men.

"Pleased to meet you, Mr Townsend," Sara said.

She couldn't help but notice that there was a sudden chill in the air. Maybe the heating had stopped working. Daniel's gaze darted between Carla and Sara. He appeared to be a man drowning in pressure; whether this was due to his wife's disappearance or if something far more sinister was afoot, remained to be seen.

"Can we get on with this, Inspector? Mr Harding and I both have important meetings we need to attend this afternoon, and time is getting on," Townsend said, an iciness to his tone and the brief smile he offered.

"Of course. I understand this must be a dreadful time for you, Daniel," Sara began. She removed her notebook from her pocket and flipped through her notes. "I wanted to assure you that we're doing all we can to find your wife. We've spoken to one of her friends and a colleague of Jessica's this morning, and certain details have come to our attention that I felt I should run past you before we go any further."

He frowned and sat back, then sat forward again and ran a hand over his chin. "What are you saying? Has someone told you that I'm lying? Because I can assure you, Inspector, nothing could be further from the truth. I have no idea what has happened to my wife. Do you really think I would be sitting here if I did? Come in voluntarily for this interview? I demand to know what people have been saying about me!"

Sara watched him closely, her sharp eyes taking in every detail. She excelled at reading people, and Daniel was giving off the aura of a man holding something back.

"Why don't we go over your relationship with Jessica?" Sara said. "From what we can gather, everyone is of the opinion that you have the perfect marriage, but that's rarely the case, is it?"

His eyes narrowed, and he cleared his throat. "I told you earlier that we had argued. I don't know a single marriage that is 'perfect', Inspector. All couples argue from time to time, but that doesn't mean that I don't love my wife. We both have extremely successful careers, which means added stress that we both have to deal with. I doubt if ours is the only marriage in Hereford that isn't perfect. Every successful couple has strains or minor issues now and again."

Townsend leaned over and whispered something in his ear.

Daniel closed his eyes, and he let out an exasperated breath. "That came out wrong. What I'm trying to say is..."

"What my client is trying to say is that he loves his wife dearly and would never harm her," Townsend jumped in to clarify for him.

Sara let the silence hang for a moment before she said anything else. "Earlier today, we had the privilege of speaking with Jessica's best friend, Laura Whitfield. She informed us that Jessica had been dealing with some personal issues lately." She paused again, then dealt her first major blow. "She also mentioned that Jessica is pregnant. Were you aware of that fact, Daniel?"

It was pretty obvious by the way he fell back in his chair that he wasn't. His mouth opened and shut several times. Finally, he found his voice and said, "What? Pregnant? No... no, she can't be. We agreed... no, she didn't tell me anything about that." His voice cracked slightly as the reality hit him. "Pregnant..." He licked his dry lips and shook his head.

"We also know about the affair she was having," Sara added to keep up the pressure. She studied him, weighing up his reaction. Then she added, "Jessica was seeing a man named Paul Grant. Did you know about that?"

For a split second, something dark flashed in Daniel's eyes, but he quickly masked it with a look of disbelief. "I knew something was off between us, but I wasn't aware that she had strayed. Paul Grant? Christ! That smug bastard..."

Sara leaned forward, her tone firm but not accusatory—yet. "When did you find out? About the affair?"

Daniel shook his head and appeared confused. His voice barely above a whisper, he sneered, "I didn't. Not until now." He paused, his face contorting as he struggled to process the information. "I... I thought maybe she was just pulling away, that perhaps it was the pressure of work or something else. But I never imagined... this outcome. Next, you'll be telling me that the baby is his. Oh, shit!"

Sara shrugged. "Only Jessica can tell us that."

Carla nudged her knee under the table.

"Ah, yes, one thing I forgot to ask you when we spoke earlier."

"What's that?" he asked, still giving the impression that he was dumbfounded by the news.

"Do you have any security cameras at your home?"

"No. We both detest any kind of technology of that nature."

"Fair enough. Is there anyone else you believe we should know about?" Sara did her best to steer the conversation towards other potential leads. "Anyone from your social circles, family, or colleagues who might have had a problem with Jessica?"

Daniel sat in silence for a moment, his gaze distant as he stared at the wall behind her. "We don't have any enemies," he said slowly. He covered his face with his hands, growled, and then dropped them into his lap. "Jesus, I can't believe this is happening. How is all this going to help find Jessica? If she frigging wants to be found. That's the question you should be asking. She's cheated on me with that prat, and not only that, you've just informed me that she's expecting a baby which could be her lovers."

"We need to get to the truth. It's not every day we speak to a husband who has reported his wife missing, only to learn that his wife was potentially pregnant by her lover."

His nostrils flared, and he shouted through gritted teeth, "All right, there's no need for you to keep repeating it. Let's put our cards on the table, Inspector, shall we? Are you treating me as a prime suspect?"

"Not yet. However, unless you are willing to be more open with us, then yes, that status is likely to change."

"What the fuck? I've told you everything I know." He fell silent, and his eyes narrowed as he thought. "Wait, there is someone else on the radar you should speak to."

Out of her peripheral vision, Sara spotted Carla poise her pen over her notebook.

"Who?"

"A man called Oliver Sharpe."

"And who might he be? Another one of her colleagues at work?"

"No. Sorry, I should have mentioned him earlier; he genuinely slipped my mind, until now. Jessica handled a case for him years ago. Things didn't go well, and he's had it in for her ever since. I don't know if he's involved, but he seems a likely candidate, especially as

he's been harassing us in recent months, sending strange letters...
He's unstable."

Sara exchanged a glance with Carla. This was vital information in
Sara's opinion. This was the first they'd heard of Oliver Sharpe,
another person of interest they needed to speak to, if Daniel was to be
believed.

Carla scribbled down the name in her notebook and asked, "Do
you have any of these letters?"

Daniel nodded. "Yes, Jessica threw them in the bin, but when she
wasn't looking, I recovered them and kept them in a file... you know,
just in case anything came from his threats later. They're at home. I
can bring them in."

"You kept them against your wife's wishes or knowledge? That
seems strange, considering Jessica is a solicitor and Sharpe was her
client."

He shrugged. "What can I say? Sometimes Jessica is guilty of
being too trusting."

"We'd definitely be interested in seeing the letters. If you can
bring them in ASAP, we'd appreciate it."

"Is there anything else, Inspector?" Townsend asked. He drew
back his cuff and peered at his watch. "As I've already stated, we both
have important meetings we need to prepare for this afternoon."

"No, I think we're done here, for now. We'll track down Mr Sharpe
this afternoon and see what he has to say about all of this."

"Don't you want to see the letters first?" Daniel asked.

"Yes, that would be a good idea. I'll send a member of my team
over to collect them if you're going back to your house now?"

"Yes. I have some papers I need to pick up on my way to the
meeting."

They wrapped up the interview, but as Daniel left the room, Sara
couldn't shake the feeling that he was still hiding something. The
mention of Oliver Sharpe was useful, but Daniel's reaction to the
pregnancy and the affair left her with too many unanswered
questions.

They showed Harding and Townsend out and went upstairs.

"Craig, can you go over to the Hardings' residence? Daniel has informed us that his wife has been receiving letters from a former client called Oliver Sharpe. He's willing to hand them over to us."

"On my way, boss."

"He's going straight home."

Craig left the incident room. Sara gathered the rest of the team around for a strategy session. While she sifted through her thoughts, Carla crossed the room to the whiteboard and jotted down all the names of the people they had either spoken to or who had been mentioned so far.

"What a day, and it's not even lunchtime," Sara said.

Carla connected the threads and added their relationship with Jessica at the side of each name. The list was growing with each person they spoke to. But still, no one had been able to give them a definite idea as to why Jessica had gone missing. However, in Sara's opinion, it was time to start getting tough with some of the main players to get to the truth.

"So, we've got Paul Grant—the lover," Sara said.

She approached the board, and Carla stepped away to allow her to take over.

Sara tapped Grant's name on the board. "He was clearly involved with Jessica, and the pregnancy adds another layer. The only concern we have is that he appeared to be genuinely surprised by the news. Of course, that could be an act. There's also the niggling doubt about whether the baby is his or Daniel's. It's too early to tell yet, either way."

"My money is on Grant being the father," Carla chimed in.

"Then there's Daniel Harding—the husband. He claims he didn't know about the pregnancy or the affair, but something about his story doesn't sit well with me. We need to keep an eye on him. As yet, I can't put my finger on what's making me suspicious of him. He also revealed that there are no security cameras present at the property, which isn't helpful." Frustrated, she went back to her office to catch up on the post she'd set aside.

· · ·

CRAIG RETURNED WITHIN HALF AN HOUR. Sara cast her eyes over the letters and rejoined her team. She walked over to the whiteboard, sighed and circled Oliver Sharpe's name. "Now we've got this new player that Daniel has thrown into the mix. He's supposedly a disgruntled client with a history of harassing Jessica." She reached for the folder containing the letters that Craig had collected from Harding. "After reading through the letters he sent to Jessica, I'm going to go out on a limb and put him at the top of the suspect list. Our next priority is to speak with him, allow him to give his side of the story. Although, the contents and tone of the letters really tell us everything there is to know."

"Just a reminder," Carla said. "Don't forget about Laura Whitfield, Jessica's bestie. When we met up with her earlier, I got the impression she seemed nervous. Was that because of Jessica going missing? Or is she hiding something from us? It might be worth having a second chat with her, soon."

"I'm inclined to agree with you, Carla. I know it might seem like we're chasing our tails, revisiting certain people, like Daniel and Laura, but with nothing else to go on at the moment, needs must. I'm getting the impression that someone on this board knows more than they're letting on. Let's spend the afternoon going through the usual social media accounts and background checks. Jill, can you also look through the archives and see if anything crops up there? Apart from what we already know about Sharpe, she might have other clients out there seeking revenge."

"On it now, boss," Jill replied.

The team got their heads down, and Sara entered her office to go through her emails and complete her daily chores. However, she was distracted throughout as her gaze drifted to the file containing the harassment letters. She was eager to have a word with Oliver Sharpe, but that would keep until the morning. She wanted to be more prepared with research notes to hand before she tackled him in person.

.   .   .

AT FIVE-FORTY-FIVE, exhausted, Sara pulled the team together for a final time that day. "We've worked hard today, folks. Thank you for all the effort you've put in on the case so far. Let's call it a day and start afresh in the morning."

The team shut down their computers and left the office. Only Carla and Sara remained. Carla stretched her arms over her head and yawned.

"That's how I feel. This has been a strange investigation right from the word go, hasn't it? I know we've spoken to most of the people on that board, but it feels like we haven't got very far at all. No one has any inclination as to what might have happened to Jessica. All we've really got on that front is Daniel's word on what took place, which was all rather vague." Sara scratched the back of her neck. "Nope, I refuse to keep going over it. We need to go home and get some rest. Shit, I forgot, you haven't got a car. Do you want me to drop you off?"

"No, it's fine. Des is due to finish at six, I'll cadge a lift with him. You carry on. I'll switch the lights off when I leave."

"I feel awful leaving you here on your own."

"Don't. You look done in. Get home and have a rest."

Sara yawned. "I won't argue with you. I'll see you in the morning. I hope Des doesn't keep you waiting too long."

"Ditto. Enjoy your evening."

Sara picked up her keys and handbag and left the office. She bumped into Des in the corridor. "Hi, Carla's in the office, waiting for you. How are you?"

"Everything is fine with me, you?"

"It could be better. No doubt Carla will fill you in during your drive home."

"I'm sure she will," he called after her as she ran down the stairs.

When she arrived home, twenty minutes later, Mark was making a start on the dinner. She slipped off her shoes and coat and wandered into the kitchen. "Something smells nice. How was your day?"

He leaned over and kissed her while he continued to stir the bolognese sauce. "Hectic. What about yours?"

"The same. Can I lend a hand?"

"Nope, it's all under control. Do you want to open a bottle of wine?"

"I could do with a drink tonight. I shouldn't get called out... I suppose one wouldn't hurt."

He put the wooden spoon on the plate and held out his arms. She walked into them.

He kissed her on the top of the head. "Sorry for being such a grouch this morning."

"Don't worry, I'm used to it," she replied, smiling up at him.

His mouth turned down at the sides. "I don't want you to be used to it. I was out of order. I'm sorry."

She placed a hand on his cheek. "Honestly, it doesn't matter. Everyone is entitled to have an off day now and again."

"But since the operation, that's happening all too often. I've been chastising myself all day about the way I treated you. I would have given you a call, except I've had back-to-back appointments all day."

Sara put a finger on his lips. "It's fine. It's forgotten about. Do I have time to get changed?"

"Yes, I'm about to put the spaghetti in. Unless you'd rather have pasta instead?"

"Spaghetti will make a change. I'll be right back."

She made a fuss of Misty the cat, and then ran upstairs to remove her work clothes. After slipping into her leisure suit, she brushed her mid-length brown hair and spotted a few grey ones at the side, above her ear. "Great, that's all I need." She groaned and went back downstairs.

Mark was dishing up their meal. Sara poured them both a glass of red wine and laid the table.

"Don't take this the wrong way," he began after they'd both sampled their meals. "But you look exhausted."

She smiled. "It's been a tough day. In and out of the station, questioning friends and family of a woman who has gone missing."

"Oh, bugger. Who? Or can't you tell me?"

"One of the top solicitors in the area. It's all rather mysterious. Do you mind if we don't talk about it?"

"Of course. I'm here if you need me. Have you spoken to your father today?"

"Damn, no, it completely slipped my mind. I'll give him a call after dinner. This is wonderful, as usual. So much better than anything I could knock up within twenty minutes of being home."

He rolled his eyes. "Creep. I have to admit, it is rather good. I swilled out the jar of Marmite and added that."

Sara laughed. "I've never thought about using that before. It works. You look tired, too. Are you sure you're not doing too much after your surgery?"

"I'm fine. Being busy helps to take my mind off it."

After their meal, Mark insisted he would clean up the kitchen. Sara took her glass of wine through to the lounge and called her father.

"Hi, Dad. Sorry I haven't got back to you sooner. I've had my back to the wall all day."

"I appreciate how busy you are, love. We can talk another time if you're too busy to listen."

Sara sensed the hesitation in his voice. "No, it's fine. I have a few notes to make later. Go on, tell me what's wrong."

"Nothing is wrong, as such." He gulped and sighed.

"Dad? I know when something is on your mind. Tell me. Oh God, you're not ill, are you?" After losing her mother a few years ago, Sara and her sister, Lesley, had been concerned about her father and had made a point of keeping in regular contact with him. Admittedly, Lesley was the one who was more reliable on that front.

"Stop that! No, it's nothing to worry about. Umm... Margaret and I wanted to invite you and Mark to dinner on Sunday. The invitation will be extended to your sister as well."

"How wonderful. Is it your anniversary?" Sara racked her brain. For the life of her, she couldn't remember when her father and Margaret had begun seeing each other.

"No, it's nothing like that. We'll see you on Sunday around midday, then, yes?"

"We'll be there. I'll try and call you later on in the week. You know where I am if you need me in the meantime."

"I do. You worry too much. Enjoy what's left of your evening. Say hi to Mark for me."

"I will. Love you, Dad."

"I love you, too, my darling daughter."

She ended the call with unexpected tears bulging.

Mark entered the room. "Hey, is everything okay?"

"Yes, he's invited us for Sunday dinner. Lesley will be there too, and Margaret, of course."

"That'll save us cooking. I'm up for it. What's the occasion?"

"There isn't one. Something is brewing, though. I can sense it."

He laughed and topped up their drinks, then flopped onto the couch beside her. "Are you guilty of playing detective with your father again?"

She laughed. "Possibly."

They chinked their glasses and cuddled up to enjoy the next part of a thriller series they'd been watching for a few weeks.

4

The following morning, Sara and Carla paid Oliver Sharpe a visit. His residence was a far cry from the upscale home of the Hardings—an old, run-down house on the outskirts of town. The front garden was cluttered with junk and overgrown weeds. The man who answered the door looked like he hadn't seen a razor or, indeed, a shower in days. His eyes were wild and darted between them suspiciously.

"Oliver Sharpe?" Sara flashed her ID.

He nodded.

"I'm DI Sara Ramsey, and this is my partner, DS Carla Jameson."

"So? What do you want?" he snapped hoarsely.

Sara guessed he'd just woken up. "We're investigating the disappearance of Jessica Harding," she replied firmly. "We understand you've had some... contact with her recently."

Oliver snorted. He crossed his arms as if wishing to erect another barrier between them. "That woman ruined my life. You think I'm sad she's gone? Nothing could be further from the truth. I hope she never comes back."

Sara cocked an eyebrow. "Can we come in? Speak to you privately about this?"

"No, here will do. Say what you've got to say and bugger off."

"If you insist. Why don't you tell us exactly what happened between you and Jessica?"

Oliver hesitated, his gaze still shifting between them but also behind them as well. "She was my solicitor. I trusted her, and she stabbed me in the back. I lost everything because of her. My business, my home... every-sodding-thing."

"You sent threatening letters," Carla pointed out. "Why?"

Oliver shrugged, unmoved by the statement. "I might have done. It doesn't mean I've touched her. They were words, that's all. I wanted her to feel what I felt—betrayed. But I haven't laid a finger on her. I don't know where she is, and I don't care."

Sara wasn't convinced. "We've read the letters; they were sent when you were angry. Am I right?"

"What kind of dumb question is that? I told you, it's because of her that I lost everything. Look at this place. Do you really think anyone in their right mind would choose to live in such a shithole? Too right, I was angry when I sent those damn letters. I don't regret sending them, either. Just because I threatened her with all sorts, it doesn't mean I would carry out such threats."

"You expect us to believe that, having read those letters?" Sara pressed.

"I couldn't give a shit what you believe. She obviously didn't have a problem with them, or she would have dobbed me in to the police long ago. She didn't, so I'd advise you to run along and badger someone else about her whereabouts because, I repeat, I haven't seen hide nor hair of her in months. Not since she ruined me, or put the extra nail needed in my coffin. Now, if you'll excuse me, I have to get ready for an interview. I probably won't get it, but at least I'm trying." He took a step back and slammed the door in their faces.

Sara and Carla returned to the car.

"Shit! I thought he might be a bastard to interview, but I'm not getting the impression he's behind her disappearance," Sara said. "What about you?"

"It's hard to tell. If he's that desperate, there's no telling what he's capable of."

"Gut instinct is telling me he's trying to get his shit together, his life back on track. I think this is a case of a wounded man spouting off, who hasn't considered what the outcome of his bitterness might be."

"If you say so."

Sara narrowed her eyes and said, "You don't sound convinced."

"I'm not, but it's what you think that matters during an investigation."

"That's a load of bullshit and you know it. I value your opinion. I just think we're barking up the wrong tree and liable to waste a lot of valuable time if we go back and confront him."

"Like I said, it's your call. Where do you want to go next?"

"I think we should drop by Laura's place of work, catch her off-guard and have another chat with her."

"Sounds good to me. She works in an estate agent's office, a few minutes' walk from Jessica's office."

Sara drove into town and parked in the supermarket car park again. This time, she chose to leave the vehicle in the open air instead of going underground. They passed the courtyard café, and Sara was tempted to drop in for a caffeine top-up. "As enticing as it might be, we'll see how things go with Laura first. We can always stop off for a quick coffee afterwards."

"As long as you're buying; I'm skint. My salary doesn't allow for the odd coffee here and there, not when we have to dip into our pockets to pay for them."

"All right, grumpy knickers, I'll pay."

Carla shrugged. She pointed out the estate agent's office at the end of the row of shops in the town centre.

"Is this new? I can't say I've noticed it before."

"A year or so, I think."

"It seems out of place to me."

"Me, too. Maybe they're trying to think outside the box."

Sara smiled and pushed open the door. The young blonde woman sitting at the first desk came to greet them.

Sara flashed her warrant card. "Is Laura Whitfield here today?"

"Oh my. Yes, she's in her office. I'll get her for you." The woman scampered to the back of the open-plan office and returned with Laura a few moments later.

"Oh, hello, Detectives. Nice to see you again." Laura peered over her shoulder and kept her voice down. "I wasn't expecting to see you so soon. Please tell me you've found Jessica?"

"We haven't. Forgive the intrusion. Would it be okay if we had a quick chat with you?"

"Can't it wait? I'm at work on a tight schedule, and my boss is a bit of a tyrant. He despises us having personal visits at work."

Sara sensed that Laura was trying to give them the brush-off. "Sorry, it's important, otherwise we wouldn't be here."

Laura exhaled an impatient breath. "Very well. You'd better come this way. But I can't spare you long, not without getting my boss' permission."

"That's fine."

Laura led the way to her office and quickly closed the door behind them. "Sorry, I only have one extra chair in here. One of you is welcome to use mine; I don't mind standing. It'll make a change from me sitting on my backside all day long."

Carla rejected the offer and opened her notebook as she stood next to Sara, who chose to sit. Laura sat in her chair and fidgeted under Sara's gaze.

"How can I help?" Laura asked.

"We just wanted to touch base with you again, having spoken to everyone else. I don't suppose you've heard from Jessica since she went missing, have you?"

"No, not at all. I wouldn't have asked you if you'd found her as soon as I saw you today, would I?"

"Ah, yes," Sara said, playing along. Her idea for interviewing Laura was to try to tie the woman into knots, sensing that she knew more about what was going on than she had told them so far. "Am I right in thinking that you were the last person to see Jessica before she disappeared?"

Laura picked up a pen and twiddled it between her fingers. "I don't know, you tell me. What about Daniel? Didn't he see her that evening? I presumed he was due home not long after I left her."

"Possibly. The thing is, Laura, having spoken to all the parties concerned, experience tells me that you've held something back from us. Have you?"

Laura's cheeks turned beetroot, and she bit her lip until it bled. Then she broke down in tears.

"Laura, what's wrong?" Sara's heart raced, but she was keen to get the woman to trust her. She softened her voice and said, "Please, if you want Jessica home safely, you have to tell us what you know."

"Oh God. I didn't want to deceive you. Please forgive me," she sniffled.

Sara opened the packet of tissues she always kept in her pocket and offered one to Laura. "No one is going to think badly of you, providing you tell us the truth."

Laura blew her nose and muttered an apology, "I'm so sorry. I thought Jess would be back by now. I can't imagine what she must be going through if someone has kidnapped her. She's pregnant, for fuck's sake. How could someone do this to her? She doesn't deserve to be treated this way. You have to find her."

Sara raised an eyebrow. "With respect, we're trying to do just that, but the trouble is, we're reliant on what other people tell us. If certain people insist on keeping vital information from us, then that is bound to make our job somewhat harder."

"I know. I'm so sorry. I didn't mean to..."

"Apology accepted. Now, can you tell us the truth, Laura?"

"Yes, you're right, there is something I didn't tell you before... I didn't want to get anyone in trouble."

Sara leaned forward. "What is it, Laura?"

"Jessica wasn't only afraid of Paul," Laura whispered and paused for several more seconds before she delivered another blow. "She was afraid of Daniel, too."

"Why would she be afraid of her husband?"

"She confided in me that they had been arguing more than usual. She didn't go into the nitty-gritty detail of every argument they'd had, but I could tell something was seriously wrong with their marriage. Saying that, I didn't think he would hurt her, but now... I'm not so sure."

Sara and Carla exchanged concerned glances. This was a major revelation Sara hadn't expected to hear.

"Why didn't you come right out and tell us this before?" Carla demanded, her tone sharp.

Sara winced at her partner's aggressive words. "Carla is right. You should have been honest with us from the outset."

Laura wiped away her tears. "I'm sorry. I know that now. I just thought Jess would be back. I thought she had walked out on Daniel to teach him a lesson and that everything would be all right the next day. I never expected her to still be missing. I was scared to tell you the truth. Scared of what Daniel would say or do if he found out I had spoken to you. Please, please forgive me."

Sara inhaled and exhaled several breaths to calm herself. "All this has done is waste our time and, dare I say it, probably put Jessica in more danger."

Laura shrieked then clasped a hand over her mouth. "Oh no, don't tell me that. I thought I was doing the right thing... protecting Daniel."

"We could charge you with wasting police time, Laura. It would appear that we're the only ones taking Jessica's disappearance seriously."

"You're not. I've lain awake all night, thinking about what might have happened to her. I felt sick when I got up this morning, physically sick. She's my dearest friend, and now I have to live with the fact that I've betrayed her by not telling you the truth."

Sara had heard enough. She despised being made a fool of. "I'll need to have a word with my boss, see if she wants to press charges against you. Good day, Miss Whitfield." She stormed out of the office with Carla close on her heels. She heard Laura wailing, pleading for forgiveness until they left the premises.

Carla struggled to keep up with her. "Hey, slow down." She tugged on Sara's arm and spun her to face her. "You're allowing her to get to you. Come on, Sara, you're better than this."

"Am I? What the fuck, Carla? What are we doing? Every person who has spoken to us has lied in one way or another. They're taking the piss out of us. Either Daniel wants our help to find his wife, or he doesn't. If it's the latter, then does that mean he's responsible for Jessica going missing?" Sara was so wound up that she stamped her foot several times.

Carla laughed. "I'm sorry. You can be hilarious at times. Come on, let's get that coffee you hinted at earlier. Umm... it might be my suggestion, but don't forget you offered to pay."

Sara growled at her partner. "As usual. Yes, I need to take time out."

"On one proviso."

"What's that?"

Carla smiled. "We don't discuss the case."

Sara held out her hand, and Carla shook it.

"Deal," they said in unison.

By the time they reached the station, after their detour to the café, Sara had calmed down, even though her mind was swirling with numerous possibilities. She brought the rest of the team up to date as soon as they entered the office.

"So, to sum this mess up, we've got Jessica, who is pregnant, guilty of having an affair with Paul. She's also scared of her husband, Daniel, according to her best friend, Laura. Now, here's the thing. Laura hid the truth from us because she feared what Daniel's reaction would be if he found out she'd told us." She raised a hand. "Don't ask. Her logic is beyond me. All we can be certain of is that the suspect list is growing, and the truth is buried deep in a tangle of lies.

Which is frustrating the hell out of me. I've still got a feeling that there is much more for us to uncover. What we can't do, or should I say, what I refuse to do, is keep revisiting these people, just to get the next snippet of information they decide to drip-feed us."

"I can understand that, so what should we do instead?" Carla asked.

"I'm not sure. If Daniel is behind Jessica's disappearance, we're lacking any hard evidence to tackle him with. We've got several suspects, but again, no concrete leads. However, there are motives aplenty. Nevertheless, my gut is still telling me there's something missing."

"Will digging deeper into Jessica's personal life help?" Carla asked.

"I think we need to grill more of her friends and family, people she interacted with on a regular basis."

"What about her colleagues?" Jill asked.

"Let's start making a list. Search the usual SM accounts and check the archives to see if anything regarding the law firm is lurking in them."

They spent the rest of the morning doing the research, then over lunch, which Craig volunteered to collect from the baker's across the road, discussed what they'd found.

5

After they'd eaten, Sara and Carla headed out to interview Jessica's colleagues at Richards and Grant Solicitors. The office was sleek and modern, with high-end furnishings and the quiet hum of efficiency. The receptionist smiled and welcomed them as they entered.

Sara produced her ID and asked to speak to the person in charge.

"Oh, that would be Mr Richards. I'll have to check if he's available. Can I ask what your visit is about?"

Sara smiled at the woman in her thirties. "We'd like to chat with him about a case we're dealing with."

"Very well. I'll be right back. Take a seat."

Sara declined the offer and, instead, checked out the noticeboard in the reception area. Her gaze was immediately drawn to the firm's charges. They expected their clients to pay an eye-watering two hundred and fifty pounds for a mere letter sent from one of the partners.

"Pricey," Carla whispered.

"We're in the wrong business. Can you imagine how many cups of coffee you could buy at our favourite café if you worked here?"

Carla elbowed her in the ribs. "Cheeky cow. Seriously, how the heck can people afford these prices?"

"I'm betting only a select few can. Don't forget Oliver Sharpe lost everything he had. At least, that's what he told us."

The receptionist returned and asked them to follow her through to what appeared to be a conference room, where a smartly presented man in his fifties was waiting for them. He rose from his seat and shook their hands.

"Edward Richards at your service. I'm one of the firm's founding partners."

From the research the team had carried out that morning, Sara already knew that fact. She also knew that he was a shrewd and successful solicitor in his own right.

"Thank you for meeting with us, Mr Richards," Sara said. "We're here to ask a few questions about Jessica Harding, more specifically, her role at the firm."

Edward gestured for them to sit. "I've been expecting a visit, Inspector. We're all very concerned about Jessica. She's one of our top lawyers, and this situation has been a shock to all of us."

"How would you describe her relationship with her other colleagues?" Sara asked, immediately cutting to the chase.

"Professional," Edward replied, although Sara picked up on a slight hesitation in his voice. "Jessica was, or rather is, always very focused on her work. If I were to sum her up, I'd say she was ambitious, driven to succeed."

Sara shuffled forward in her seat. "We understand she was involved in a personal relationship with Paul Grant, one of the senior partners here. How did that affect her standing within the firm?"

Edward's warm smile vanished, and his expression darkened. He shifted uncomfortably. "I only learnt of the affair recently. I wasn't happy about it. Paul assured me that it wouldn't affect their work. Thankfully, from what I can tell, he kept his promise. They tried to be discreet about it, but it didn't take long for the rumours to circulate. Some of their colleagues didn't approve."

"Can I ask who, and why they didn't approve?" Sara winced, unsure whether her question would come across as being naïve.

He paused to stare out of the window, which overlooked the car park at the rear of the property. "Hmm... the main instigator was Helen Marsh," Edward admitted. "She's another partner here. She was actually close to Jessica for a while. But when the relationship with Paul became general knowledge around the office, things drastically cooled between them. Helen is a strict professional—she's never been one to tolerate workplace relationships that might damage the firm's reputation."

"Is Helen the type to hold a grudge against Jessica?" Sara asked.

Edward sighed and took a moment before answering, as if he were choosing his words carefully. "I don't think so. But Helen is a tough woman. An utter professional who expects the best from everyone, and Jessica was no exception. If Jessica's performance slipped because of personal issues, Helen wouldn't have hesitated in giving her a warning."

"Even though she brings in a lot of business for the firm?"

"As I've already stated, Helen expects everyone to conduct themselves professionally on these premises. If Jessica wasn't one of our best employees, I fear she would have been shown the door as soon as the rumours surfaced."

"That seems a bit extreme. Would it be possible to speak with Helen to get her take on Jessica's disappearance?"

"If she's free. I can ask if she has time to see you."

"If you wouldn't mind. Thank you."

He left his seat, looking relieved that the interview was over, for now.

Once he closed the door, Carla leaned over and whispered, "Bit of an archaic attitude, isn't it?"

"I suppose solicitors have a reputation to uphold. Maybe Helen Marsh is old school. From what I can recall, she's in her forties."

"That's still young. I thought you were going to say she was in her sixties, closer to retirement age."

The door opened, and Edward nodded. "Helen can spare you ten minutes before her next client is due. Please, come with me."

They followed him down the length of the corridor, and he introduced them to the brunette woman who remained seated behind her grand mahogany desk. The office was neat, nothing out of place from what Sara could tell. She offered her hand and invited them both to take a seat.

Helen smiled and dismissed her associate. "You can leave us now, Edward."

"Of course." He closed the door.

Sara and Carla sat.

"I've been told why you're here. Edward has made you aware that I haven't got long." Helen thrust her shoulders back, making her seem even more in authority than Sara had first thought.

"He has. In that case, I'll get straight to the point. We're trying to get an idea of what Jessica is really like, if you wouldn't mind sharing your views with us?"

"I'll do my best. Jessica Harding is a talented solicitor with a bright future ahead of her."

Sara detected a chill in her tone. "I sense a 'but' coming, am I right?"

Helen nodded and continued, "She's been very distracted around the office lately. Her work has been slipping, and I've had grave concerns about her focus."

"By distraction, do you mean because of her relationship with Paul Grant?" Sara asked.

Helen's eyelids fluttered shut for a moment. Sighing, she said, "I believe that was the main issue, yes. Everyone knows how I feel about office romances. In my experience, nothing good comes from them at all. Paul should have known better, but Jessica... well, let's just say I expected more from her. As women, I'm sure you'll agree, we all have to work harder than our male counterparts in order to succeed. I recognised her potential when she first began working here. She was foolish to let her personal life interfere with her career. In this business, that's a dangerous mistake to make."

Sara studied Helen for a moment, considering her words. "Did you ever confront Jessica about her behaviour?"

"I most certainly did," Helen said without hesitation. "A few weeks ago. I told her she needed to get her priorities straight. She was upset, of course, but I don't regret it. She needed to hear the truth, although I stopped short of telling her that I thought she was screwing up her career."

"Did you know her well enough for her to confide in you? Did she confide in you about her marriage? Any possible problems with Daniel?" Carla asked.

Helen shook her head. "No, over the years we have become slightly closer, but not enough for her to confide in me, obviously. It was clear something was going on. She seemed tired and was exceptionally distracted. I assumed it was because of the relationship she had with Paul. I have since learnt from Paul that she was pregnant." She shook her head in disgust.

"Thank you for that. We're aware that she's had an ongoing issue with one of her former clients, Oliver Sharpe. Did she talk to you about that?"

"Only briefly. I told her to ignore him and get on with her life. We've all had cases that haven't gone the way we'd expected them to. Going to court can, and often does, work against us and our clients. Nothing is written in stone in our line of business. Our clients are informed of the risks from the outset; it's always their decision whether they want to continue."

"Do you know of any other former clients who have found themselves in the same boat and who have harassed Jessica over the years?"

"I'm not aware of any such incidents." She glanced up at the clock on the wall behind her. "Time is marching on, Inspector."

"Okay, perhaps you can tell us if anyone else in the firm has any issues with Jessica?" Sara asked, changing tactics.

Helen's expression hardened. "We're a competitive firm. There's always going to be rivalry between the employees. I think you'll find that's the same in most law firms. I can tell you that everyone likes

Jessica." She paused to take a breath. "She's ambitious, much like me when I started out. I suppose that's why I was harder on her than the others. However, not everyone appreciates her approach. But that's the nature of the job."

"Who didn't like her?" Sara pressed.

Helen hesitated, then sighed. "There was tension with a junior associate, Ethan Clarke. He was one of Jessica's protégés, but things had turned sour between them lately. I don't know the details, but Jessica stopped mentoring him a few months ago. I believe Ethan took it personally. I'm sorry, I really must call a halt to this meeting now. My client is a stickler for timekeeping, and so am I, for that matter. I hope the information I have given you will help you bring Jessica back to us. We miss her, despite the mistakes she's made recently."

Sara and Carla exchanged a look and stood.

Sara reached out and shook Helen's hand. "Thank you for your time and for being so open with us. We appreciate it. Do you think it would be possible for us to speak with Ethan?"

"I don't see why not, unless he's with a client. I'll take you back to the reception area. I can collect Mr Jarvis at the same time."

"Thanks, that'd be great. Perhaps, on the way, you could point out which room is Jessica's office?"

They left the office, and Helen opened the door on the right.

"This is hers." Helen strode off ahead of them.

Sara stuck her head into another neatly presented office. She noticed a photo of Daniel and Jessica on the desk. She sprinted to catch up with Helen and Carla.

"Katrina, the officers would like to have a word with Ethan if he's available."

"Ah, that might be a problem. I've just this minute shown his latest client through to his office."

"We can wait. It's not an issue for us."

Helen nodded, then walked towards a man in his late fifties, who was flipping through a magazine in the waiting area. "Nice to see you again, Mr Jarvis. Come through to my office." She smiled as she passed Sara on the way back up the corridor.

"Ethan shouldn't be too long," Katrina said. "I could make you a coffee while you wait."

"Thank you. That would be most welcome."

Once the receptionist had left the area, Sara whispered, "Whilst Helen seemed abrupt, I didn't sense that she was holding back, did you?"

"That's a first, with this lot. I agree. She was open and honest with us and has even given us the name of yet another suspect."

Sara laughed. "Easy, tiger. Let's not get too carried away, not until we've spoken to Ethan. It's quite a small practice. It makes you wonder how Jessica and Paul ever thought they could keep their affair a secret."

"Lust will do that to you." Carla sniggered.

"Voice of experience talking, eh?"

Carla's cheeks reddened. "Hey, you're the one who set me and Des up, don't forget that."

Katrina brought them both a coffee and placed the tray on the small table in front of them. "Help yourselves to milk and sugar."

"Thanks. How long is Ethan likely to be, do you know?"

"Ten or fifteen minutes at the most."

"Thanks again." Sara added the milk and a spoonful of sugar to each mug and handed one to her partner. They drank their drinks in silence. Sara made a few notes, mainly writing down her observations so far regarding what they had established from speaking with Edward and Helen.

She glanced up ten minutes later when she heard two male voices coming up the hallway. The receptionist caught her attention and raised her thumb, letting her know that Ethan had finally finished his meeting with his client.

"I'll be in touch soon, Mr Smalling. Take care." The young man held the door open, and his client left the building.

"Ethan, these two officers would like a word with you."

He spun around and frowned. "Do I know you?"

Sara and Carla stood.

"I don't think we've had the pleasure. I'm DI Sara Ramsey, and this is my partner, DS Carla Jameson. Would it be convenient to have a quick chat with you, Ethan?"

"About?"

"Jessica Harding."

He rolled his eyes. "We'll take this in my office. This way."

They followed him a short way up the corridor into a smaller office that was also impeccably neat and tidy. Sara noticed there were certificates on the wall to the right, but they were too far away for her to be able to read them.

"Take a seat," he instructed. He swivelled his executive chair to face him and slipped into it. "I heard that Jessica has gone missing. How can I help?"

Sara and Carla sat in the chairs provided, and both withdrew their notebooks.

"We understand that you worked closely with Jessica," Sara said. "Can you tell us a bit about that?"

He fiddled with his tie and then shuffled some papers on his desk. "Yes, that's right. She was my mentor when I started at the firm. I'll be forever grateful for the help she's given me from day one."

"And yet, we've been told that your relationship has changed recently," Sara said, the words coming out sharper than she'd intended. "May I ask why?"

His gaze dropped to his hands and then up at her again. "I... don't know. Things got tense between us. She started distancing herself from me. I thought maybe I wasn't living up to her expectations, so I backed away from her."

"Did you have a disagreement?" Sara asked, determined to chip away at his cool exterior.

Ethan swallowed hard. "Not exactly. I... I made a mistake on one of her cases. It wasn't a big deal, but she got really upset. After that, she stopped giving me the big projects. I guess she lost faith in me."

Sara leaned forward, her eyes narrowing. "Did you lose faith in her?"

Ethan blinked, clearly taken aback. "What? No! I mean, I was frustrated, sure. But I didn't have anything against Jessica. She was under a lot of pressure. I just figured she was dealing with stuff I didn't know about."

"Did you know about her personal issues? The affair with Paul Grant?" Sara asked, watching for any reaction.

Ethan's eyes widened. "No, I didn't know anything about that. I mean, there were rumours about her and Paul, but I thought that was office gossip. I didn't think it was true."

"Have you ever felt like Jessica was keeping something from you? Something that might have put her in danger?" Sara pressed.

Ethan shook his head quickly. "No, nothing like that. I just... I don't know. I feel like I let her down. But I swear I don't know where she is."

"What about any of her clients? We know about Oliver Sharpe and the trouble she's had with him. Is there anyone else you can think of who has been making a nuisance of themselves?"

"Now you're asking. I didn't know about Sharpe; saying that, I'm not surprised. We worked on his case together."

"Is that the case you messed up?" Sara asked bluntly.

He bowed his head in shame. "Yes. Oh God, you're not telling me he's got something to do with her disappearance, are you?"

"Let's just say he's on our suspect list, along with others."

"Blimey, how many others?"

"I'm not prepared to divulge that kind of information. Is there anyone else you think we should be talking to?"

He stared at the wall for several moments and then shook his head. "I don't think so, but then, I've already told you, I haven't worked with Jessica for a while, not since the Sharpe case."

"What happened with that case?"

"I'm not sure whether I'm allowed to tell you—client confidentiality and all that. I'd need to run that past Edward before I open my big mouth."

Sara smiled. "If you wouldn't mind."

"What? Now?"

Sara's smile broadened. "Yes. There's no time like the present."

He huffed his way to the door and returned a few moments later to take his seat once more. "Okay, he's given me the go-ahead. Umm... I'm not sure where I should begin."

"I find at the beginning always helps."

"Okay. It was my role to do all the research needed on the company Sharpe worked for, and what I found was very worrying. I can't share specific details with you. I'm not allowed to, Edward said to keep the details to a minimum."

Sara shrugged. "I suppose we could get a search warrant if we feel it's needed in the future. Please continue."

His eyes widened. "That's up to you. I need to work hard to put things right around here, so I have no intention of going against Edwards' instructions."

"You've made that perfectly clear," Sara said, her annoyance obvious.

"There's really nothing more I can tell you. We went to court and used what we'd found against the company. It backfired on us, big time, and we walked out of there with egg on our faces. Jessica blamed me, even though I ran everything I had uncovered past her. She agreed to use it in court, so I felt the onus should have remained with her. But no, muggins here took the fall for her, me being the junior associate."

"You sound bitter, Ethan."

His eyes widened. "Shit! Wouldn't you?"

"Possibly. Did you tell Jessica you were sorry?"

"For what? I presented the facts, and it was up to her to go with them or not. Maybe she was too wrapped up in juggling her personal life to think it through properly before we went to court. I refused to take the blame and told her that. The rift between us widened after that."

"I can understand why. Is there anyone else around here with a grievance with Jessica?"

"I didn't have a *grievance* with her. I was in the right and she was in the wrong, end of."

"You've made your point. Can you answer my question?"

"No, I mean yes. No, I can't think of anyone else. We're all hopeful that Jessica will come back to us soon. Deep down, I have always admired her. She's strong and determined. I pity the bugger who has abducted her." He laughed.

Sara felt the need to slap him down. "Forgive me, but I don't regard someone being abducted as a laughing matter."

"Er... yes, you're right, I'm sorry."

"We'll leave the discussion there for now, but we might need to question you more in the future."

He shrugged. "If you think it will help, then fine." He showed them back to the reception area and opened the door for them. "It was a pleasure meeting you, ladies."

Sara noticed the change in his demeanour, as if he were relieved to see them leave.

"You, too. We'll be in touch if we have any further questions for you. Here's my card, in case you think of anyone else we should interview."

"I'll let you know," he said and slipped the card into his pocket.

The door closed behind them, and Sara let out a frustrated growl as they crossed the road towards the car. "Fucking liars, the lot of them."

"What? Even Helen and Edward?"

"I think Helen might be the only exception. I've never trusted a solicitor I haven't worked with professionally. I can understand why now."

"I feel your frustration, and I can double it. They might have come across as concerned, but I think it was all a front. It's all so bizarre."

"Yeah, that's what is troubling me as well. What if she isn't missing and has just packed a bag and taken off somewhere?" Sara thumped her thigh. "No, I doubt if she would have done that, not after leaving her car in the garage. What the fuck is going on here?"

By now, they had reached the vehicle, and they both glanced back at the premises they had just left.

"Someone knows something, but who?" Carla asked.

"Get in. Let's get back to the station and do yet more digging."

"All we're doing is going round and round in circles. It's bloody driving me nuts, and we're only in the preliminary stages of the investigation."

"Hang in there." Sara started the engine. "Someone is bound to slip up soon, and when they do, we'll be there waiting for them. I've changed my mind about returning to base. We should stay out on the road. Let's see what Jessica's parents have to say about all of this."

"Want me to ring Jill to get their address?"

"Please." Sara reversed the car and headed towards the exit. She paused before joining the traffic.

"I've got it." Carla ended the call and punched the postcode into the satnav.

6

The afternoon sun filtered through the large windows of Winston and Margaret Cartwright's spacious countryside home. It was a stark contrast to the gloom that hung over the investigation. Sara hoped Jessica Harding's parents would give them fresh insight into their daughter's life—especially in light of her recent troubles. If they were aware of what had been going on.

When they pulled up, Mr Cartwright was pottering in the cottage's front garden. He eyed them with concern as Sara pushed open the gate. "Hello, can I help you?"

Sara flashed her ID and introduced herself and her partner.

"Ah, we expected you to visit us sooner. My wife is in the kitchen, baking. Come round the back."

"Sorry for the delay in coming to see you. We've had a lot of people to interview over the last couple of days. How are you and your wife holding up?"

"We're not, not really. We're doing anything and everything we can to keep busy, including praying for our daughter's safe return."

"I can imagine. We're here to assure you that we're doing all we can to bring your daughter home safely."

"And how long will that last? Before you hit a brick wall and close the case? I've heard the police are so busy that missing person cases are being pushed aside, only being given a cursory look over these days."

"I'm not sure who has given you that idea, sir. Nothing could be further from the truth," Sara assured him.

The garden at the rear of the property was in pristine condition, despite the time of year. January was always a bleak month to be out in the garden. It must have been Mr Cartwright's passion, as well as a good distraction while his daughter was missing.

"Come in. Wipe your shoes thoroughly on the mat first, if you would. You can keep them on. The kitchen floor is tiled, and the rest of the downstairs is floorboards. I'd better take mine off, otherwise Margaret might be tempted to string me up and then you'd have a murder case on your hands, as well as a missing person case." He joked, but the laughter never met his eyes.

"We wouldn't want that, would we?" Sara smiled.

The door led into a very clean utility room. When they entered the kitchen, they found Margaret putting a tray of scones in the oven.

"Oh, you startled me, Winston. I thought you said you'd be a couple of hours out there. I was about to have a read." She set an alarm on the front of the oven. When she turned around, she gasped, realising her husband wasn't alone. "Sorry, I didn't know anyone else was here. Why didn't you say something?" She eyed her husband and shook her head.

Winston introduced Carla and Sara to his wife. Sara was impressed he got their names right.

"Well, don't just stand there. Take them through to the lounge while I make us all a nice cup of tea."

"Would it be any trouble for you if we had coffee instead?" Sara asked.

"Not at all. Go through, I've boiled the kettle, so I won't be long."

Mr Cartwight showed them through the hallway into a large lounge. The dominating features were the inglenook fireplace on one wall and a bay window with a padded seat on the opposite side of the room. It was a warm, cheerful room, not what Sara was expecting, given the Cartwrights' age.

"Take a seat. My wife and I usually sit here on the sofa." He gestured for them to sit opposite.

Sara sat, and Carla withdrew her notebook before sitting next to her.

"Have you lived here long?" Sara asked.

"About thirty years. We decorated this room last year. Jessica helped with the design. It's not something Margaret and I would have chosen for ourselves, but we're used to it now and pleased with it."

"I love it. It's homely and welcoming with a few modern touches."

"Yes, that's what Jessica was aiming for when she asked her designer friend to come up with something different. Margaret wasn't too impressed with it to start with. I didn't mind, but then men don't really have an eye for interior design, do they?"

Sara smiled. "Possibly."

He shot out of his chair and opened the door wider to allow his wife to enter with the tray. "Had you left it another half an hour to visit us, I could have offered you a freshly baked scone. Will a short-bread do instead?"

"That's perfect. You're spoiling us," Sara said.

"Help yourselves to sugar and milk."

Sara did the honours and passed Carla a china mug. They both declined a biscuit for the time being.

Margaret plucked a tissue from the box next to her and held it in preparation. Winston appeared to stiffen beside her, his face set in a hard, unreadable expression.

"Mr and Mrs Cartwright, thank you for meeting with us. First of all, I'd like to assure you that we're doing everything we can to find Jessica. As I told your husband, the reason we have delayed visiting you is that we thought it was important to interview Jessica's friends and colleagues first. We're hoping you can fill in the gaps for us and tell us more about your daughter. Do you know what Jessica was going through before she disappeared?"

Margaret dabbed at her eyes with the tissue, her voice shaky when she spoke. "Jessica... she's such a strong woman. Independent. But I... I knew something was wrong."

Winston, however, remained silent, his gaze fixed on the two mugs left on the tray. Sara noticed his clenched fists and the way his jaw continuously tightened and slackened. It was clear that the disappearance of his daughter was deeply affecting him, but he seemed determined to hold it together.

"Care to enlighten us as to what you mean when you say, 'something was wrong'?" Sara asked gently, leaning forward.

Margaret sniffed and glanced at her husband as if seeking his approval to continue. After a long, uncomfortable pause, she spoke again. "Jessica hasn't been herself these last few months. I suppose she seemed distant. Whenever we spoke, she brushed off our questions about her personal life. She usually confided in us about everything, but lately... I've had the impression that she was hiding something."

"Did she mention any specific problems? Do you think it had to do with her husband, Daniel, or more to do with work issues? Or something else entirely?" Sara asked.

Margaret shook her head and wrapped the tissue around the fingers of her right hand as she thought. "No. She wouldn't discuss the issue and insisted everything was fine. But I could tell. A mother knows when her child is in trouble."

Winston finally spoke, his voice low and steady. "Recently, Jessica hasn't confided in us, not the way she used to. Not since she married that man." His words were sharp, and Sara immediately picked up on the tension.

"You're referring to Daniel Harding?" Carla prompted.

Winston's face darkened. "It should be obvious who I'm referring to. I've never liked him. I always felt he wasn't right for Jessica. I know you'll probably think that a father never believes the man his daughter marries will ever be good enough for her, but it wasn't like that. He has always come across as smooth and, dare I say it, calculated. He came from money, just like us, but there was something... off about him. I've always felt like he was hiding something. I didn't hold back either. I told Jessica as much, but she wouldn't listen. She loved him, and there was no talking any sense to her."

Margaret placed a hand on her husband's arm as if to calm him. "Winston, please... Don't get yourself into a state about this."

But Winston went on, determined to have his say. "I wouldn't be surprised if he had something to do with this," he said coldly. "I always knew he would bring her nothing but trouble."

Sara and Carla exchanged a quizzical look. It wasn't the first time they'd heard concerns about Daniel, but hearing it from Jessica's father added weight to the suspicion that Daniel might not be as innocent as he claimed to be.

"Did Jessica ever mention any problems in her marriage?" Sara asked. She took a sip from her coffee now that it had cooled slightly.

Margaret hesitated before answering, her voice barely above a whisper. "No, but... I could sense something was wrong between them. When they came to visit, there was always a tension. I presumed he was here under sufferance. They tried to hide it, but I could tell."

Winston shook his head. "He's a control freak. Always has to be the one in charge of a situation. I don't know what he did to her, but he's the one to blame for this, I'm sure of it."

"We're exploring every possibility, Mr Cartwright," Sara said. She hesitated a second or two, undecided whether she should reveal all to Jessica's parents. "Were you aware of anything going on at the law firm?"

They both frowned and shook their heads.

"Such as?" Winston asked. "Workwise? Are you telling us she was in trouble? Going to lose her job? If so, this is the first we've heard about it. She loved working there. Has always been the utter professional."

Sara swallowed and decided to show all her cards and reveal the truth. It was the only way they were going to find out what was going on. "No, I believe her job was safe. However, it has come to light that Jessica was involved with one of her colleagues."

"What? Involved how?" Winston demanded. "You're not trying to tell us that she was having an affair with someone, are you?"

Sara sighed and nodded. "I take it you didn't know?"

Margaret gasped, her hand flying to her mouth as fresh tears filled her eyes, while Winston's face flushed with anger.

"An affair?" he repeated in disbelief.

"Yes," Carla confirmed. "With a man called Paul Grant. They've been seeing each other for a little while, but according to her friend, Laura, Jessica had ended the relationship. We're not sure when, but it would appear to have been just before she disappeared. We're trying to determine if this played a role in what happened to her."

Margaret was trembling now, tears streaming down her cheeks. "Oh, Jessica... why didn't you tell us?"

Winston's hands clenched into fists. "I don't care about this Paul Grant. All this proves is that she wasn't happy in her marriage. Happy people don't stray. It's Daniel. He's the one who's been controlling her life. If there's anyone responsible for her disappearance, it's him."

Sara took note of Winston's certainty. It backed up what she'd been thinking, but she was aware that personal bias could cloud someone's judgement. She needed to ask more objective questions.

"That's one aspect we're looking into at present. What about Jessica's work?" Sara shifted the focus. "Did she ever talk to you about any issues she might be having at the law firm? Colleagues she didn't get along with?"

Margaret sniffed, composing herself as best she could. "It's hard to say now that you've told us about the affair. She kept that fact from us. However, what I can tell you is that she loved her job, but... recently, she seemed more stressed than usual. She didn't go into details, but she did mention in passing once that things were tense at work. She told me she was working on some big cases, and I think the pressure was getting to her."

"Do you know if she had any conflicts with her colleagues?" Carla asked.

Margaret shook her head. "No, it wasn't a subject she raised that often. Maybe she wanted to protect us from that."

Sara leaned back in her seat and thought about what they'd learned. Jessica's parents had provided more insight into the tension between Jessica and Daniel, but there were still gaps. The mention of her stress at work could point to other issues, perhaps even conflicts with people like Helen Marsh or Ethan Clarke, but there was still no clear link to her disappearance. No motive as such.

"What about a case that had gone wrong? Did she tell you about that?"

"I can't remember her telling us about that, can you, dear?" Margaret asked her husband.

"No, not that I can recall. I know she mentored a young man for a while. She really didn't tell us much about that, either. I brought the subject up once, but she chose to steer clear of it and spoke about something else instead. Did something drastic happen?" Winston asked.

"A male client they were representing apparently lost everything and blamed Jessica for letting him down. Daniel gave us some letters the man had sent to their house. They threatened revenge."

Winston opened his mouth to speak, but Sara raised a hand and continued.

"We've since spoken to Oliver Sharpe and, while he remains on the suspect list, I don't think he's capable of doing anything bad to her. In our experience, when someone puts their intentions in writing, they rarely follow through."

"I can understand you thinking that, but if this man has motive, shouldn't that count against him?"

"Like I said, we haven't dismissed him as a suspect, not yet."

"But you think there are other prime candidates, apart from him," Winston said.

Sara nodded. "Is there anything else you can tell us? What about former boyfriends or partners? Has Jessica ever had any issues with anyone she's broken up with in the past?"

Margaret shook her head. "No, our daughter remained friends with them all. She isn't the type to stop speaking with someone. She's not that petty."

Sara finished off her coffee and then rose. "Okay, then we must press on. I'll leave you one of my cards. If anything else should come to mind, will you let me know?"

Winston stood and accepted the card. "We will. We can understand you wanting to get on with the investigation, but please, please remember what we've told you about Daniel. I don't think he's to be trusted. Can't you drag him down the station, hold him in a cell for a couple of hours and then interrogate him?"

"We've spoken to him twice already; once was at the station with his solicitor in attendance."

"Don't leave it there. You need to keep the pressure on him. He's a tough cookie, but I think there are a lot of secrets buried beneath the surface."

"We'll take that on board. Thank you both for seeing us at such short notice."

Margaret stood as well, and wrung her hands. "Please... find her," she whispered, her voice breaking. "Bring our Jessica home."

"We're doing everything we can, I promise you," Sara reassured her, though she could feel the weight of Margaret's desperation. It was a feeling she had become all too familiar with over the years when speaking to relatives in similar situations, and yet it never got any easier.

"Take care of each other. Hopefully, we'll soon be in touch with some good news regarding your daughter."

Winston showed them to the front door and shook their hands. "Thank you for all you're trying to do for us. Please, I'm begging you, don't be fooled by her husband."

"Duly noted. Don't worry, sir."

They returned to the car. Once inside, they stared back at the cottage. A shell-shocked Winston was standing on the doorstep, watching them.

Carla exhaled loudly. "Well, the parents, or should I say, the father, didn't hold back. I'm sensing that if we gave Winston a rope with a noose on the end, he'd be first in line to kick the box beneath Daniel's feet away."

Sara nodded, her mind still racing with the new information. "He's convinced Daniel is behind this, but we still haven't got anything concrete to link him to Jessica's disappearance. And the affair throws a spanner into things—who knows what else Jessica was hiding?"

Carla sighed.

Sara drove back to the station. "You know, for a woman with a picture-perfect life, Jessica sure has a lot of secrets. The more we dig, the more complicated this case gets."

"Everyone around her is a potential suspect," Carla murmured. "The husband, the lover, the bitter ex-client, the colleagues... everyone had something to gain or lose by getting rid of Jessica. Everyone except her parents—Margaret's devastated, but Winston? I think he's more focused on blaming Daniel than finding out what really happened. That's telling in itself."

"I think it's time to pull Daniel in again," Sara suggested. "Winston's got a point—if Jessica was afraid of him, that's a red flag we'd be foolish to ignore."

Carla nodded. "I don't think we have much choice but to bring him in. Perhaps having another word with Paul Grant wouldn't go amiss either. Something about him still feels off."

As they drove back into town, Sara's thoughts drifted to Jessica's life, now a puzzle with pieces scattered across the people who claimed to know her best. Each person they interviewed added yet another piece, but the full picture remained elusive.

And Sara had the sinking feeling that the darkest secrets were still buried, waiting to be uncovered.

7

The darkness was the first thing Jessica Harding had become accustomed to. It had been days—maybe even weeks—since she'd last seen sunlight. Time blurred together in the cold, damp space she had been trapped in, the musty smell of old wood and mildew constantly filling her lungs. She had counted the hours at first, trying to make sense of the passing days by the subtle changes in the air and the sounds filtering through the cracks in the walls. But now, she had lost track of what day it was.

Her hands, bound with rough ropes, ached from the tightness. She had stopped trying to free herself long ago; her attempts had made the rope tear into her skin, leaving raw, angry welts around her wrists. The gag in her mouth made it difficult to breathe, and her lips were cracked and dry. She had been given water occasionally—just enough to keep her alive. Food had also been scarce. Nothing but scraps pushed through the door when her captor could be bothered. Life was so miserable that she wanted to seek God to end it.

The only light in the room came from a single, bare, low-wattage bulb hanging overhead, casting long, eerie shadows across the rough wooden floor. The room was small, claustrophobic, with no windows and only one door. The door—her only chance of escape—was locked from the outside, and she had heard the heavy scrape of a bolt sliding into place the last time her captor had left.

Her mind kept drifting to Daniel. Questioning if he knew she was missing. Was he looking for her? Or had he given up, assuming she had left him? And what about the baby? Jessica's hand, as best she could with her bindings, rested on her stomach, a small, comforting gesture despite the terror that gnawed at her insides.

A noise outside the door jolted her from her thoughts. The sound of footsteps on the concrete floor sent her heart racing. She tried to steady her breathing, but panic surged within her. The door creaked open, and a figure stepped inside.

Her captor.

The figure moved deliberately, staying just out of reach of the light. Jessica's pulse quickened as she strained to see more, her body rigid with fear. She had seen her captor before, but the shadows had always obscured their face. She didn't know if it was a man or a woman—only that they moved with purpose, always calm, careful never to utter a word.

They approached slowly, stopping just in front of her. The figure knelt and reached out to check the ropes around her wrists, tightening them further. Jessica winced as the rough fibres bit into her already raw skin.

For the first time, her captor spoke—a low, measured voice that sent chills down her spine.

"You shouldn't have come back," the voice hissed. "You ruined everything."

Jessica's heart skipped several beats. She tried to speak, to ask what they meant, but the gag muffled her words into incoherent responses. Her eyes widened in confusion. She hadn't come back from anywhere. What did they mean? She didn't understand.

Her captor's hand grabbed her chin, forcing her to look up. "I warned you," the voice continued. "But you didn't listen. Now you're going to pay for it."

Jessica's breath came in shallow gasps as she stared at the shadowed figure. Her mind raced, trying to piece together what they were talking about. Did she know this person? Had she wronged them somehow?

But there was no time to make sense of it. Her captor stood abruptly and turned, leaving the room as quickly as they had entered. The heavy bolt scuffed across the door, locking her in once again.

Listening to the footsteps fading into silence, Jessica's thoughts spiralled. She couldn't remember. She didn't know what they meant about 'ruining everything'. What had they meant? Was it something to do with work? Or, further back, something that had happened in her past? Who were they? So many questions ran through her mind and no answers, none that made any sense anyway.

The fear gnawed at her, deeper now, but she knew she had to stay calm. Panicking wouldn't solve anything; it would only make things worse. She closed her eyes, focused on steadying her breathing, and tried to think clearly.

Her mind went to Daniel again. She could only hope that he was looking for her, that someone knew she was missing and was doing everything they could to find her. But the longer she remained in this godforsaken place, the more she feared no one would come, and that she would die here, in the darkness, without ever knowing why.

The hours—or days, she couldn't tell—passed in a blur. The next time her captor entered the room, they brought something with them. A phone. Jessica's eyes widened in surprise as the person placed it on the floor in front of her, the screen already lit up. She could see the faint glow of numbers—her husband's number.

Jessica's heart leapt. Were they letting her call Daniel? Was this a trick? Something else to punish her with if she jumped at the chance to speak with her husband?

Her captor crouched beside her again and removed the gag from her mouth. Jessica gasped for air, her lips cracked and bleeding. She glanced up at her captor, eyes wide with fear and hope.

"You're going to call him," the automated voice instructed. "Tell him you're leaving. Tell him not to look for you."

Jessica stared at the phone, her mind reeling. *What? Why would I do that?* Her thoughts raced. *Does Daniel know something? Is my captor trying to frame him?*

"I can't," Jessica whispered, her voice hoarse from dehydration.

Quick as a flash, her captor's hand shot out, grabbed her hair and pulled her head back sharply. Pain shot through her scalp, and she cried out.

"Call him," they repeated. The robotic voice sounded cold and detached.

Hands trembling, Jessica took the phone and stared at the number. Daniel. Her husband. Her mind screamed at her not to do it, but the fear and pain proved to be too much for her in the end. Sensing that she had no choice, and with shaking fingers, she pressed the button to dial. The phone rang once. Twice.

Then Daniel's voice answered, distant and confused. "Hello? Hello? Who is this? My God, Jess, is that you?"

Tears sprang to Jessica's eyes at the sound of his voice. But before she could speak, her captor leaned in closer, their breath hot against her ear.

"Do it," they whispered. "Or I'll kill him, too."

Jessica's breath caught in her throat. With her fear increasing, she had no choice.

"Daniel," she croaked, forcing the words out. "I... I'm leaving. Don't look for me."

There was silence on the other end. "What? Jess, where are you? What's going on?"

"I'm leaving," Jessica repeated, her voice breaking. "Don't try to find me. Please."

Before Daniel could respond, her captor snatched the phone from her hand and ended the call. The screen went dark.

Jessica's heart shattered into a million pieces. She had just lied to the one person who might have been able to save her. And now, she had no idea what was going to happen next.

Her captor stood, their figure looming over her in the dim light. The gag was shoved back into her mouth. "Good girl," they murmured. Then turned and left the room, leaving Jessica once again in the suffocating darkness.

As the bolt slid into place, Jessica let out a sob. She was trapped, alone, and completely at the mercy of someone who wanted her to disappear forever. Worse than that, she had no idea why.

8

After they arrived back at the station, Sara mulled over contacting Daniel for a third time while she went through her post. She was at her desk when Carla pushed open the door and stood in front of her, the office cordless phone in her hand, her eyes wide with alarm.

"You're not going to believe this," Carla said breathlessly. "Daniel just got a call from Jessica."

Sara shook her head in disbelief. "What? Are you sure?"

Carla nodded. She put the phone on the desk and showed Sara the call records she'd brought with her and pointed at the digits at the bottom of the sheet. "It's there. It came from an unknown number. Jessica told him she was leaving. She warned him not to look for her. But here's the thing—Daniel said she sounded terrified. He felt she was being forced to say it."

Sara's mind raced. If Jessica had called, it meant she was still alive —but being held against her will. Her captor had made her lie, likely to throw Daniel—and the police—off the scent. Were they closing in on the truth?

"We need to trace that number," Sara said. She placed the pile of letters she was dealing with in her in-tray and tore around the desk.

"Get the team on it now. If we can locate where that call came from, we might be able to find her."

Carla was already ahead of her, typing furiously into her mobile. "I've got Jill working on it. But Sara... we have to tread carefully. If Jessica is with someone dangerous, and they know we're closing in, they might panic. They could hurt her."

"I hear you." Sara knew Carla was right, but the urgency in her chest wouldn't let her stay still. Jessica had reached out, however controlled it might have been, and that was a sign she was still fighting for survival. Or was she? *Or is this a stunt by Daniel? A setup? Is he fearing that we're closing in on him?* Sara sighed and shook her head, confused about what to believe for the best. As they joined the rest of the team in the incident room, the scenarios kept coming into Sara's mind. *Jessica was being held by someone who had control over her, someone with a motive strong enough to keep her alive, yet hidden. And now, they were trying to isolate her further by pushing Daniel away.* Even though the doubts were growing, she still kept coming back to Daniel's possible involvement, and she knew better than to discount any misgivings that arose.

"This could change everything," Sara muttered to Carla. "The fact that she called means that the captor is playing some sort of game. We've got to figure out who benefits from Jessica disappearing without a trace—and why they're keeping her alive."

"There's something more. I can see the uncertainty in your eyes."

Sara ran her hand around her face. She perched on the desk behind her and placed her palms flat against her thighs. "What if someone is trying to put us off the scent?"

"I don't understand," Carla said. She scratched her head and added, "Daniel said that despite what Jessica mentioned about leaving him, he felt someone was forcing her to say it."

"I know... oh God, I've got this niggling doubt that I can't bloody shift."

Carla pulled out a chair behind one of the spare desks and asked, "About Daniel?"

"Yes... oh, I don't know, perhaps."

Carla shrugged. "Maybe you're right to have doubts. I haven't forgotten what his father-in-law had to say about him."

"Yep, I wasn't thinking about that, but yes, that fact kind of backs up my claim, too. What if Daniel is feeling the pressure and either got one of his friends—or, worse still, paid someone—to make that call?"

"So there was a paper trail?" Carla said, nodding her agreement.

Sara heaved out a breath. "Either that or I could be talking out of my arse. Let's face it, it wouldn't be the first time I've suspected a husband of being behind the murder or abduction of his wife over the years."

"And I doubt if it will be the last, either. You're right, we can't take what he says as gospel, not if there are lingering doubts in our minds."

"It's not just me, then? Are you sensing he's behind this as well?"

"I wouldn't go as far as to say that, not in a court of law, if it came to it. However, we've both said that something doesn't add up from day one of this investigation. And the more we dig, the more our suspicions grow against Daniel."

"But... we've got no evidence or proof against him."

"Which is crucial in our business, isn't it?"

"Yep. Jill, how's it going?"

"I'm in touch with a tech analyst. He's working on triangulating the location. It's not easy, but we're getting some pings. Looks like the signal was bouncing between towers just outside Hereford."

"Keep at it." Sara rubbed at her chin as she thought. "We need to know exactly where that call came from." She stood and approached the whiteboard. Carla joined her. Sara picked up the marker and added the call as a fresh development. She also jotted down Jessica's parents' names and drew a line back to Daniel.

"Whoever took Jessica has enough control over her to force her to make that call," Carla said, pointing at Daniel's photo. "Is he as innocent as he's trying to make us believe? Or is someone out there, intent on using him as a pawn in their game? Someone smart enough to use psychological warfare, telling Daniel not to look for her. But why?

What are they afraid of? Jesus, my head is spinning with all the probabilities."

"Playing devil's advocate for a moment, maybe it's not about fear," Sara replied. "Perhaps they're buying time. Maybe their intention is to keep Daniel from pushing the investigation forward, allowing them to stay hidden longer."

Carla tapped the whiteboard with her finger. "And we can't forget about the pregnancy. If the captor knows about that—and if it's not Daniel's baby—they could be using it as leverage. I don't know. I'm just throwing anything and everything into the mix."

They both stared at the board in silence for a moment, considering the suspects they had lined up: Daniel Harding, the husband with everything to lose; Paul Grant, the lover who may or may not be the father of Jessica's child; Helen Marsh, a colleague with motives tied to professional rivalry; Ethan Clarke, a frustrated junior associate who Jessica had blamed for screwing up a case. Finally, Oliver Sharpe, the embittered ex-client who blamed Jessica for losing everything.

Jill shouted and punched the air, gaining Sara's attention. "We've got a lead. Coordinates are coming through now, boss."

Sara and Carla shared a look. They had a location. This could be it!

The address led them to the outskirts of Hereford, a run-down industrial area that appeared abandoned. The road was quiet, lined with old warehouses and crumbling brick buildings. Sara's gut twisted into a large knot, which meant they were getting closer.

Sara's stomach churned when they pulled up in front of one of the larger, more isolated warehouses at the back. The building looked like it hadn't been used in years, but there was a faint, eerie sense of activity about it—as if something sinister were hidden beneath the surface.

"Where the hell is the backup?" Carla asked, her voice tight with anticipation. "They should be here."

"They're on the way," Sara replied, scanning every inch of their surroundings. "But we can't wait. This is down to us. If Jessica is in there..."

Carla nodded, understanding.

They couldn't afford to lose precious time.

Quietly, they approached the entrance, their hands resting on their Tasers. Sara was thankful that Carla had finally seen sense and taken her Taser training. The door was slightly ajar, and Sara, holding her breath, pushed it open. Inside, the air was thick with dust, the faint smell of rust, decay and urine filling the space. The light was dim, filtering through the cracked windows above.

They moved through the ground floor of the warehouse, careful of the route they took through the littered interior. The warehouse was quiet—too quiet. Then a noise sounded off to their right. Faint but distinct. A shuffle. Someone was inside.

Sara placed a finger to her lips and motioned to Carla. They split up, increasing the gap between them, both walking towards the source of the disturbance. Sara's heart drummed against her ribs. She rounded a corner, her gaze probing every shadow.

Then she saw it—an old door, half-hidden behind a stack of pallets. It was slightly open, and beyond it, the whisper of movement. Her pulse quickened. She signalled for Carla to join her.

They drew their weapons and, with one swift motion, Sara kicked the door open.

Inside, the room was pitch-black, but in the corner, tied to a chair, was a woman. Jessica. Her face was pale, her eyes wide with fear and exhaustion. A cloth was stuffed in her mouth, preventing her from crying out for help. Her hands were bound, her clothes torn and dirty, but she was alive.

"Jessica!" Sara rushed to her side and holstered her Taser. She knelt and removed the gag then tugged at the tight rope. "I'm sorry, this might hurt."

Jessica's voice was hoarse, barely a whisper. "It doesn't matter. I want it off. Please... don't let them... come back..."

"Who are they? Do you know?" Carla asked. She stood guard, her Taser aimed at the door while Sara continued to tug at the ropes.

But before Jessica could answer, a loud clang echoed through the warehouse, the unmistakable sound of metal against metal. Someone else was out there.

Sara's blood ran cold. With the rope removed, she pulled Jessica to her feet. "We need to go. Now."

But just as they reached the door, a shadowy figure appeared, blocking their exit.

Jessica clutched Sara's arm. Sara stood in front of her and aimed the Taser.

Jessica gasped and whispered in a terrified voice, "It's them..."

Sara and Carla closed the distance between them, their Tasers aimed at the intruder, but the figure didn't flinch. Instead, the person took a step forward with deliberate calm.

"I warned you," the voice said. It was cold and familiar.

Sara recognised it. It belonged to a person high on their suspect list.

9

The figure stepped forward and Sara tightened her grip on the Taser. However, the person's face was still cloaked by a shadow. Jessica's terrified whimper echoed in the cold warehouse air. Carla shuffled closer, her own Taser poised, ready to fire.

"Stay right there. Don't move," Sara commanded, her voice steady but edged with urgency. "Put your hands up. Now!"

The figure stopped but didn't raise their hands. Instead, they tilted their head, the faintest hint of amusement in their posture.

"I warned you, Jessica," the voice said, low and controlled. "You never should've tried to leave."

Jessica clung to Sara, her body trembling, her breaths shallow and erratic. "Please... don't believe him. He's dangerous."

The figure moved closer, out of the shadows and into the sparse light available, and Sara's breath caught in her throat. Paul Grant. His handsome face looked weirdly contorted, and his blue eyes were filled with a strange intensity.

"Paul?" Carla said sharply, her Taser still trained on him. "What the hell are you doing here?"

But Paul didn't respond immediately. His gaze fixed on Jessica, his expression unreadable. The tension in the chilled air was palpable.

He let out a sinister laugh. "She didn't tell you everything, did she?" he finally said, his voice cold. "About what she was planning to do? About the life she was ready to destroy?"

Jessica's breath hitched as Paul's words cut through the silence. Sara's mind raced, trying to piece together what was playing out before them.

"Talk to us, Paul. Tell us what's going on," Sara demanded, her voice controlled but with an edge of urgency. "Why are you doing this?"

Paul's lips curled into a small, twisted smile. "None of this should have happened. It wasn't supposed to be like this. We had something, Jessica and I. Something I've never felt before. It was real. But she no longer listened to the desire that had captured her heart. She had to go back to *him*, to Daniel, to play the role of the perfect wife. It was all too easy for her to pretend I didn't exist."

Jessica attempted to move towards him, but Sara flung an arm in front of her, preventing her.

"Paul, please... you don't have to do this." Jessica's voice was croaky but full of emotion.

Paul's gaze intensified on Jessica, filled with a strange combination of anger and sadness. He shook his head and said, "I didn't want this. I didn't want to hurt you. But you forced my hand."

Carla took a step closer and asked, "Forced your hand how, Paul? Jessica did the right thing and ended things with you. She moved on. You should have done the same."

Paul let out a bitter laugh, his eyes hardening. "She didn't just end things. She was going to destroy my life. By then she knew about the baby—she was going to tell Daniel everything and set out to ruin me. All because she couldn't stand the idea that I had moved on, too. That I had got on with my life, without her."

Jessica shook her head, tears streaming down her face. "That's not true, Paul. I never—"

"Liar! Don't lie to me. You owe me the truth after the nights we spent together. The stolen moments. I thought you loved me. I had feelings for you." His voice rose, cutting her off. "You told Laura you were pregnant, and you knew it wasn't Daniel's. But you didn't have the guts to tell him, did you? Instead, you decided to cut me out of your life and pretend our great love affair had never happened. You were going to destroy me and then walk away like none of it mattered."

Sara's mind whirled. It was dawning on her just how twisted the situation had become. Paul's obsession with Jessica had taken a dark turn, and now his motives were clearer. He wasn't just holding her captive out of jealousy or anger—it was because she was going to reveal the truth about the pregnancy and expose their affair. And he couldn't allow that. Being a partner at the law firm, he had a reputation to protect.

"Paul," Sara said, keeping her tone calm, "Jessica made a choice. You need to let her go. We can work this out."

Paul's gaze flicked to Sara, and for a moment, it seemed like he was willing to consider her words. But then his expression hardened again. "You don't understand. I did everything for her. I loved her. But she betrayed me."

Carla seized the opportunity to take another step forward, her Taser still trained on his chest. "Paul, it's over. You can't keep running from this. Whatever you're trying to protect—it's not worth Jessica's life. Look at the state of her. That was down to you. Is that what you really wanted? To treat her this way?"

Before either Sara or Carla could react, he removed a phone from his pocket and held it up.

"Wait? Don't do anything rash. What are you doing, Paul?" Sara swallowed down the lump that had lodged in her throat.

Paul looked down at the phone, a glint of desperation crossing his features. "It's too late. I can't let her ruin everything. She'll tell Daniel. She'll tell everyone."

With that, he pressed a button on the phone and put it to his ear. "It's done. They're here."

Sara's stomach dropped. She knew she should have fired the

Taser and prevented him from making the call, but she was eager to find out what was going on in his mind. Carla must have thought along those lines, too. Otherwise, she would have fired her Taser as well.

"Who did you just call, Paul? Who's coming?"

Paul didn't respond. Instead, he dropped the phone on the floor and raised his hands in surrender.

Carla glanced at Sara. She nodded and held her Taser tightly. One false move and she would shoot this time, without hesitation. Her partner rushed forward and quickly secured Paul in handcuffs. All the time, his gaze remained firmly fixed on the woman he loved— Jessica. Sara read the expression that appeared to be a mixture of regret and bitterness.

"Paul Grant, you're under arrest for the kidnapping of Jessica Harding and her illegal imprisonment," Carla said. She told him his rights and led him towards the door.

As Paul was taken away, Sara released her grip on Jessica. She was shaking. Her body slumped against the wall and then slid down it.

"Jessica, are you all right?" Sara asked softly, kneeling beside her. "Don't worry, we've got him. He'll pay for what he's done to you. I'll make sure of it."

Jessica's gaze was distant. Shell-shocked, she muttered, "I didn't know he would... I didn't think he'd go this far. I just wanted to make things right."

"It's okay. It's over now." Sara helped her to her feet and then flung an arm around her waist to support her as they moved towards the exit. "We're taking you somewhere safe. But Jessica—who did Paul call? Do you know? Has he mentioned who he's working with?"

Jessica swallowed. She tried to explain, her voice trembling, "He said... he told me there were others. People who didn't want me to come back. They thought I'd tell Daniel everything."

"Everything?" Sara asked, frowning. "What do you mean? What else is going on here?"

Jessica nodded. "Everything! About the affair. About the baby. And about... the money."

Sara froze, drawing them both to a halt, her mind spinning. "The money?"

Jessica's eyes widened with fear. "Oh God, how could I have been so foolish to have ever got involved with him?"

"Jessica, you're not making any sense. I can't help you if you refuse to confide in me. Do you believe you're still in danger?"

"I don't know. I'm trying to get my head around everything. Now I know he was behind this. He used an automated voice. I didn't have a clue it was him holding me hostage, treating me like shit. Why? Why me? Paul wasn't just having an affair with me. He was involved in something much bigger—money laundering. I didn't realise it until I discovered the accounts in one of his drawers one day. He was using me. Not only me, but the firm as well. How has it come to this?"

The revelation hit Sara like a debilitating blow to her stomach. Paul hadn't just been trying to protect his personal life—he was trying to keep Jessica from exposing a criminal operation. And now, someone else was involved. Someone whose intention was evil, their goal to silence her for good.

Sara guided the terrified woman through the massive opening. The cold air hit them both with such force it took Jessica's breath away. She replaced it with several deeper breaths and whispered, "It's not over." Her voice filled with dread, and with her gaze darting around them, she said, "They're still out there. Waiting for the opportunity to silence me."

Backup had arrived, and Paul was led to the back seat of the patrol car. He glanced up, saw Sara and Jessica emerge from the building and stared at her until he finally shook his head.

Carla joined Sara and Jessica. "What now?"

"We need to get Jessica to the hospital. Make sure her wounds get seen to quickly, otherwise, there's a possibility of infection setting in. We can't have that now, can we?"

Jessica stared at the patrol car until it became a distant dot on the horizon. "I'm okay. I don't need to go to the hospital. You have to take me somewhere safe. They know I was held here. Please, we need to get out of here in case they come looking for me. I'm not safe... I'm not safe... please, get me out of here. Now!"

Sara threw a comforting arm around her shoulder. "No one is going to hurt you. You're safe with us."

Jessica's eyes filled with fresh tears. "Am I? Can you be sure of that? I thought I was safe in my own home, but I wasn't. They got to me. I can't go back there... they'll come for me again. Now that Paul's in custody... they won't be so lenient on me next time. Oh God, the baby. None of this is any good for my baby. Yes, perhaps you're right. Please, take me to the hospital. I need to ensure my baby is all right."

Sara nodded. They walked towards the car, and another patrol car arrived. She had a word with the officers inside the vehicle and instructed them to escort them to the hospital. Hoping this would give Jessica added peace of mind.

On the way, looking through her rear-view, Sara observed Jessica sitting in the back seat. "We should call Daniel and let him know that you've been found."

Jessica shook her head and locked gazes with Sara in the mirror. "Not until I know my baby is safe, please."

Sara sighed and nodded. "Okay, if that's what you want."

"Thank you." Jessica placed her hands over her slight bump and stared out of the window at the green fields they were passing. "I can't believe you found me, but I fear things are far from over."

"I can't emphasise this enough, Jessica: you're safe with us. We combatted Paul without too much effort. Trust us."

"I'll be forever grateful to you for coming to my rescue."

The car fell silent during the rest of the ten-minute journey to Hereford Hospital. Sara stopped off at a small shop to pick up a drink and a sandwich, which Jessica nibbled on. At the reception desk, Sara showed her ID to the woman in charge and explained the situation to her.

"Oh, gosh. Okay, in that case, let me have a word with someone and see if we can process her quickly." She glanced at Jessica and gave her a sympathetic smile.

Jessica turned away, and Sara's heart sank. The last thing she wanted was for Jessica to feel like a victim. She leaned in and asked the receptionist, "Can we make sure as few people know about this as possible? Jessica doesn't want to be treated like a victim."

The receptionist gasped, and a hand covered her chest. "Oh yes. I totally agree. I'd feel the same in her situation."

Sara smiled. The receptionist left her desk and trotted up the corridor, where she knocked on a door halfway up. She returned with a female doctor.

"This is Doctor Harper. She's agreed to squeeze Jessica in."

The doctor approached Jessica and asked all three of them to accompany her back to her office.

"Would you rather do this alone, Jessica?" Sara asked.

"No. If it's okay with the doctor, I'd like you both to be there with me."

"Of course. If that's all right with you, Doctor?"

"It is. Why don't we check if the baby is okay first? If you'd like to slip behind the curtain."

Sara and Carla took a seat while the doctor examined Jessica. Sara sent a text to Jill at the station, making her aware of where they were and what had happened. She also told Jill that they would return to base ASAP, once the doctor had given them the go-ahead to leave. A thumbs-up emoji came back from Jill.

The curtain was drawn back, and Jessica sat in the vacant chair next to Sara.

"What's the verdict, Doctor?" Sara asked.

"I would like to get a scan sorted, if that's okay with Jessica?"

"Thank you. I'd rather know if the baby is all right."

"Let me see what I can arrange for you. Then we'll patch up your wrists. You were lucky, the bindings weren't as tight as they could have been. There was a genuine risk of your circulation being cut off."

"I feared the worst. I tried to get out of my bindings in the beginning, but the more I tussled with them, the tighter they became."

"I don't think there's any real damage done. We'll get the scan sorted and your wounds patched up then send you on your way. You're a very lucky lady, after the trauma you've been through."

"I'm aware of that. Thank you, Doctor."

The doctor left the room.

Sara placed a hand over Jessica's. "Stay positive. I'm sure the baby will be okay."

"I don't know how you can be so certain. He gave me scraps to eat and water every now and again. A foetus needs nourishment to grow, doesn't it? Especially in the early stages. Let alone the stress I've been through... I've got a feeling it's too late to save it—him or her." She covered her eyes with her hands and sobbed.

Sara patted her arm. "Come on. You need to remain strong. Don't give up hope, think positively."

"I can't. What's there to think positively about?" Her breath came out in short, sharp bursts. "I've got nothing left. I cheated on my husband with a man who—there are no other words for it—used me. Why does everything have to be about men bettering themselves at the cost of the females around them? Why did he start the affair with me? Don't answer that, we all know why. I detest them all. Using bastards, the lot of them."

Sara shook her head. "Honestly, there are still some decent men left in this world; granted, not many. I'm sorry Paul used you. You have my word that we won't let him get away with it. You're a solicitor, you know how these things work."

"I am. And I can tell you, in my experience, I've seen many solicitors getting away with murder, not literally, but close to it, over the years. We're all aware of how corrupt the justice system is."

"I'd rather not think about it. Other solicitors have been able to turn the system on its head, for sure, but that's when another solicitor hasn't been involved. I sense this case will be different. I'm determined to make sure it is. We'll throw the book at him if we have to." Sara passed Jessica a tissue to dry her eyes.

"I have one question. I'm not sure if you're going to be able to answer it or not."

"What's that?" Sara tilted her head and asked.

"Why do you think he surrendered so easily?"

"Maybe because we had the Tasers aimed at him?" Sara said, although the thought had also crossed her mind on her journey back to the car.

Carla shrugged. "Because at the end of the day, he showed what a coward he is?"

"The jury is still out on that one for me," Sara said. "Maybe he'll tell us when we interview him later."

"What will happen to me? I won't feel safe going home. I'm not even sure if Daniel will want me back, if he knows about the baby. Does he?"

"Yes. We had to tell him," Sara confirmed.

Jessica bowed her head in shame. "I suppose Laura told you, did she?"

"That's right. All I can tell you is that everyone has been really worried about you."

She glanced up and asked, "Even Daniel?"

Sara smiled. "Yes. I'm not saying it's going to be easy going forward, but if your marriage is worth fighting for, then it's got to be worth a shot, hasn't it?"

The door opened, and the doctor returned, putting an end to their conversation. "We've got ten minutes to get you down the corridor and in for a scan before their next appointment is due. I have a wheelchair waiting outside."

Jessica left her seat and joined the doctor at the door.

"Shall we come with you?" Sara asked.

"No," Doctor Harper said. "You can wait in the hallway. We shouldn't be long. We'll be straight there and back. She'll be safe with me. I've asked a security guard to accompany us."

"Thank you," Jessica murmured. She eyed Sara with uncertainty etched into every crevice of her makeup-free face.

"You'll be fine. We won't be far away."

The four of them left the room together. Sara watched the doctor and the security guard wheel Jessica down the hallway. Her heart skipped a beat when they turned the corner. Sara immediately started pacing the floor.

"Oh bugger, here we go," Carla complained and flopped into one of the chairs outside the doctor's room.

"What? Sod off, you know what I'm like when I'm nervous. We're taking a risk, letting her out of our sight."

"If you thought that, why the hell didn't you insist on us accompanying her?"

"Pass. Ask me another I can answer."

Carla tutted and shook her head. "Sit down before your nervousness rubs off on me."

Sara grumbled and sat alongside her partner and removed her phone.

"Who are you calling?"

"Who are you? My boss?"

Carla pulled a face.

"Hi, Mark, it's me. Can you talk?"

"I've got another patient due in five minutes. Is anything wrong?"

"No. I was calling to say I might be late home tonight."

"Okay. How late?" He sounded distracted.

"I'm not sure. The good news is we found the missing woman. I have to interview the man who was holding her captive, and I also need to sort out somewhere safe for her to stay."

"Yes, yes. Okay, tell me about it later. I have to go now."

He abruptly ended the call. She stared at her mobile.

"I take it he was busy," Carla said. She leaned over and jabbed the END button.

"I presume so, even though he told me he wasn't."

Carla frowned. "Is everything all right between you?"

Sara chewed her lip. "I wish I knew. I think it is, but then there are days when I feel he's trying to avoid me."

"Have you had any form of intimacy since his operation?" Carla came straight out with the question that knocked Sara sideways.

"What? Of course we have."

Carla closed one eye and asked, "Actual sex? I'm not talking about foreplay here. I'm asking if you've done the deed."

"Do you have to make it sound so sordid?"

"I did? Stop going all around the houses and answer the question."

Sara ran a hand over her face and groaned. "Do I have to?"

Carla gasped. "Which means I was right. You haven't, have you?"

Clearing her throat, Sara said, "I'm not comfortable talking about my sex life, or should I say, lack of it."

"I can take a hint." Carla removed her phone from her jacket pocket and fiddled with her latest fixation: her puzzle app.

Sara rang the station to check with Jill that Grant had been processed. Jill confirmed that he was waiting in his cell for Sara to return.

"We shouldn't be too long. To save a bit of time, can you touch base with the witness protection peeps? Make them aware of the situation and ask if they have somewhere Jessica can stay for a few weeks. If the answer is no, can you ring round all the hotels and see what's available?"

"Leave it with me, boss."

Sara dropped her phone into her pocket, stood and stretched her arms above her head, then, without realising she was doing it, she started pacing again.

Her partner's tutting alerted her. She walked further down the hallway to read a noticeboard until Jessica returned with Doctor Harper and the security guard. Sara was pleased to see them, but also apprehensive about hearing the news.

"How did it go?"

Jessica smiled up at her from her wheelchair. "The baby is fine. It has a strong heartbeat."

Delighted, Sara bent down to hug her. "Wonderful news. Can we get her back to the station now?" she asked Doctor Harper.

"A nurse tended to her wounds, which turned out to be superficial in the end. And, as Jessica wasn't missing long enough to cause too many problems, I'd say, she's free to go." The doctor faced Jessica. "Keep in touch, I mean it. Call me if there are any other issues during your pregnancy."

"You're very kind, thank you, Doctor."

The security guard pushed Jessica to the exit, where the two uniformed officers were waiting to escort them back to the station.

10

The police station was buzzing with activity as Sara and Carla led Jessica into the building. Officers always experienced a spike of adrenaline when a suspect was arrested and, in this case, the victim had been rescued. Paul Grant may have been sitting in a cell, but the air was thick with the knowledge that the investigation was far from over. Paul's confession about the money laundering operation would shed light on an entirely new angle—one that Sara sensed could reach far beyond Hereford's borders.

After their trip to the hospital, a renewed exhaustion had swept over Jessica. In the car, she had been relaxed enough to allow her eyes to close. When they drew into Sara's parking space, she had the awkward task of waking the poor woman.

Jessica had apologised, and Sara brushed her words away with a swipe of her hand. She gently guided Jessica into a private room, away from all the noise and chaos. Jessica still looked pale, her eyes wide with the aftershock of everything that had happened. Sara and Carla exchanged a glance—they couldn't delay interviewing her. There was a lot more they needed to know.

"Take a seat, Jessica," Sara said, her voice soft but firm. "I know how exhausted you must be, but I'm sure you can understand how important it is for us to go over the finer details about what Paul said regarding the money and who else might be involved. You're safe here, but we must figure out exactly what we're dealing with. The time element could be a factor in whether we arrest only Paul or get the chance to haul anyone else in, as well."

Jessica sat down heavily in the chair, her hands trembling slightly when she placed them on the table in front of her. Her voice was shaky as she spoke. "I didn't know at first. I didn't want to know. But once I found out, it was too late."

Sara said, "Why don't we start at the beginning? You said Paul was involved in money laundering. How did you find out?"

Jessica nodded. Her gaze remained on her twisting hands as if they were mesmerising her. "He used my position at the firm. I wasn't part of it directly, but I started noticing things—documents that didn't add up, transfers to strange accounts, big amounts of money that didn't have a clear origin. At first, I thought it was just an error, but then I realised it wasn't. I went in search of the answers and found a file in his desk drawer. He'd nipped out to see a client. He didn't know what I was up to and had mistakenly left the drawer unlocked. That proved to be his downfall in the end. Or was it mine?"

"Did you confront him?" Sara leaned forward and placed her hand over Jessica's.

She pulled back and continued to twist, interlock and release her fingers nervously. Jessica swallowed hard. "I... I tried. I wanted to know what was going on. He brushed it off at first, told me it wasn't my concern. But I kept digging. The more I found, the more I realised how deep it went. Paul was just the face of it—there were others involved, people with a lot of power as well as status in the community. I couldn't believe what I was reading... he was laundering money for them."

"Who were these people?" Carla pressed. "Anyone we know? Anyone connected to the firm?"

Jessica's head rose, and her gaze darted anxiously towards the door, as if she were afraid someone might overhear. "I don't know all of their names, but Paul mentioned a few. They're businessmen—wealthy, influential men. He said they had ties to the firm's clients, and that's how they were moving the money."

Sara scribbled down notes, her mind racing. Paul's confession had already pointed them towards a broader conspiracy, but hearing it from Jessica confirmed that this was much bigger than just an affair that had blown up in their faces.

"Did you manage to copy the documents?" Sara asked. "Anything that can lead us to these people?"

Jessica hesitated and bit her lip. "I was keeping some of it. In case I needed leverage. But I left most of it at home, hidden in a place where Paul wouldn't think to look."

Sara's stomach dropped. "We need to get to your house, then. If Paul knew you had that information, he's bound to have told the others, warned them. They might search for the evidence."

Jessica's eyes widened. "You think... they might go to my house?"

"It's possible," Carla agreed. "If they suspect you know something, they could be trying to find those documents. If they discover them, they'll destroy them."

Sara stood, her decision made. "I've heard enough. Time is of the essence. We need to move now. We'll take you home and get those files before anyone else can get their hands on them."

"That means I'll have to face Daniel. I'm not sure if I'm ready for that just yet."

Sara sighed. "He has a right to know you're safe and that you might both be in danger."

"Yes, of course. I need to put my selfish views aside and consider both of us in this scenario. What I think shouldn't come into it. Our safety is what matters, Daniel's and mine."

"I agree."

Jeff seemed surprised to see them arrive back at the reception so soon. "Hello again, ma'am. Is everything all right?"

"Not really. We need to take Jessica back to her house. Have you got a couple of officers available who could accompany us? Strength in numbers and all that."

"Let me make the call."

"We'll be waiting in the car."

Jeff left the counter to make the call from his small office that was out of sight from the public. Sara and Carla took Jessica out to the car. They waited until two uniformed officers approached the car. Sara lowered her window to greet the newcomers.

"Thanks for this." She gave them the address and waited for them to rush back to their vehicle. Sara reversed and blew out a relieved breath, glad that they weren't going back to the house alone.

As they approached Jessica's house, the tension in the car grew thick. Jessica was in the back, staring out of the window, appearing to be lost in thought. Sara glanced sideways at Carla. They shared a knowing look, then Sara returned her gaze to the road ahead, her hands gripping the wheel tightly until her knuckles turned white.

"Knowing Jeff, he'll have organised another patrol to welcome us at the house," Sara broke the silence.

Carla nodded, her eyes scanning the streets as they neared Jessica's upscale neighbourhood. "Paul's been taken into custody, but if he's telling the truth about others being involved, we're running out of time. Whoever he called—there's a chance that desperation has kicked in. Who knows how that is going to present itself?"

Jessica let out a shaky breath and muttered, "I didn't mean for any of this to happen. I just wanted it all to stop."

"Hey, don't go blaming yourself for this, Jessica. You did the right thing," Sara reassured her. "But now we need to make sure we have enough evidence to take these people down. That's the only way to put an end to all of this."

Sara's relief rose when she saw the two patrol cars sitting outside Jessica's house. The uniformed officers stood by the entrance, keeping watch. Which meant that there were six of them on hand. With the officers guarding the property, it should prove to be enough of a deterrent to ward off any attempt to harm Jessica again. The house itself appeared to be as pristine as it had the first time they had visited, which seemed an eternity ago. The calm façade hiding the turmoil Jessica had been living with.

They exited the car. "Stay close to us," Sara instructed. "We'll move quickly." She ordered three of the officers to remain outside and the other three to accompany them.

Inside, the house was eerily quiet. Jessica led them through the spacious living room, past the sleek kitchen and down another hallway towards her office. She stopped in front of a large bookshelf, her fingers trembling slightly as she stood on tiptoe and reached up to pull out a thick law journal.

Behind it, a small safe was revealed, embedded in the wall.

"Paul doesn't know about this," Jessica said quietly. She entered the code. "I kept everything in here."

The safe clicked open, and inside were several thick files, neatly organised and clearly marked. Jessica handed them to Sara, her hands shaking.

"The copies of what I found: bank statements, fake invoices, offshore accounts. It's all there."

Sara hadn't expected to discover so much. She flicked through the files quickly and shook her head. It was all there—evidence of a complex and highly organised money laundering scheme. Complete with the names and numbers that would help them trace the money back to its original source.

But before they could retrace their steps and leave, a loud crash sounded from the front of the house.

Sara's heart leapt into her throat. Someone was here. She drew her Taser immediately, hoping that it would be enough to prevent whoever was out there from kidnapping or, worse still, ending Jessica's life. "Stay down," she whispered to Jessica, gesturing for her to move to the corner of the room.

Sara quickly relocated to the doorway, peeking around the corner to see the source of the noise. The officers who had been sent to protect them were nowhere to be seen. Had they left their posts outside the office to investigate the source of the noise? Her stomach clenched when she spotted two shadowy figures dressed in dark clothes entering the front door. Their movements were swift and purposeful.

"Two intruders," Sara whispered to Carla. "Both carrying guns."

Carla nodded, her Taser steady in her hands. "Our weapons aren't going to be a match for them. We need to get Jessica out of here."

"Maybe I can help." Jessica darted over to her mahogany desk along the far wall and removed a gun from the drawer.

Sara stared at the weapon. "What are you doing with that?"

Jessica grinned. "My father bought it for me and advised me to keep it handy, just in case. It's loaded, but I haven't been to the range in years."

"Hopefully, you won't need to use it."

Sara motioned for Jessica and Carla to follow her to the back door, their weapons poised.

But when they tried to move, one of the men stepped into the hallway and spotted them.

"Hey!" the man shouted, drawing his gun.

Sara reacted instantly, pulling Jessica behind her as she and Carla aimed their weapons. Shots rang out, the sound deafening in the hallway. The intruder ducked behind a large cabinet, firing blindly in their direction.

"Jessica, stay down!" Sara yelled, positioning herself between Jessica and the gunfire.

Sara held her hand out for the gun. Jessica placed it in her palm. She returned fire, her aim precise, and the man fell back. His weapon skittered across the floor. But the second intruder suddenly came into view, already moving towards them, his gun raised.

Before he could fire, the front door burst open, and the three uniformed officers who should have been outside the office stormed in, their Tasers drawn. Showing no fear, they shouted at the intruder, confusing him. His head swivelled between the officers inching towards him. The man hit the floor, Tasered by one of the officers. His weapon clattered on the marble tiles. The other officers swooped in to detain him.

Sara closed her eyes. The relief was palpable, but the adrenaline gained momentum and surged through her. The danger had passed, but the reality of how close they had come to losing everything hit hard. She turned to check that Jessica was okay.

The exhausted woman was pinned against the wall, frozen to the spot, trembling, her eyes wide with fear. "I can't believe it, they... came here to kill me. What have I done to deserve this?" She slid down the wall, covered her face with her hands and wept.

Sara knelt beside her, her voice calm but firm. "It's over. You're safe now. Come on, you're safe."

Jessica's hands dropped. She stared at Sara and said, "Am I? I'm never going to feel safe again. They came here... to my home, to silence me. To end my life."

The intruder was led away, and the officers inspecting the other man called for an ambulance to attend. One of the officers sliced a finger across his throat, letting her know that the man was dead.

Carla holstered her weapon and let out a huge sigh. "Whoever these guys are, they're not just hired muscle. They knew what they were looking for. We need to find out who sent them."

Sara nodded, her pulse racing. Paul had warned them that others were involved, and now they knew just how far these people were willing to go to keep their dirty secrets hidden. "We need to interview Paul. Force the truth out of him." She helped Jessica to her feet. "Are you okay?"

"Truthfully? I don't know. What if they keep sending bastards like this after me? I can't spend the rest of my life looking over my shoulder, wondering if someone is going to kidnap me again or even kill me."

"Don't worry, we'll bring them down. While you're in our custody, you're safe with us."

"And what happens if you don't find out who is behind this? There are dozens of names on that list. Once word gets out that I'm still alive, they might send others." She shook her head, her face etched with concern.

Sara prompted Jessica to return to the car. More officers had arrived as well as the Forensic Team. As they escorted Jessica out of the house, Sara's phone vibrated in her pocket. It was a message from the station.

We've traced Paul's call.

SARA'S PULSE quickened as she read the message. "Jesus! Let's get back to the station," Sara said, her voice steady but her mind already racing ahead. "We're about to find out who's really behind all of this."

"What about questioning Paul? Are we going to do that when we get back?" Carla asked.

"He can wait. We're going to need to act on this new information quickly, especially after what happened here. I'll get Craig and Barry to interview Paul. Maybe I should have organised that before we left the station."

Carla shook her head. "You couldn't have known this would end the way it did."

"I agree," Jessica said, finding her voice. "None of us could have known this was going to happen."

11

The drive back to the station was silent, the weight of what had just happened hanging heavy in the air. Jessica was in the back seat, pale and shaken but holding on to the files that could break the case wide open. Sara's thoughts surged while she tried to connect the dots, wondering who else might be involved and just how deep this whole scheme went.

Carla's phone buzzed, and she glanced down, her brow furrowed. She read the message. "That was forensics. They believe he was a professional. They've already run his fingerprints through the system —no match. I'm guessing it'll be the same with the other bloke, too. Professionals with a job to do. They came prepared, but we were able to stop them. This time."

"They were sent to eliminate her," Sara muttered, gripping the steering wheel tightly. "They wanted to make sure Jessica didn't talk, and if we weren't there..."

Carla nodded grimly. "It's clear that whoever's behind this has serious resources. We've got a name now. That's the hard part done. The fact that it's someone close means we've been missing a key player all along."

"Let's hope we're not too late to haul this person in."

They pulled into the station. Sara waited for the other officers to surround them before they quickly ushered Jessica inside. They led her to a secure room. Two officers remained with her, while they figured out what their next move should be.

Sara and Carla headed back upstairs to the incident room. Sara's mind focused on the new lead they had.

The atmosphere in the incident room was tense. Jill informed them that Barry and Craig were interviewing Paul Grant. Carla prepared the coffee, while Sara approached the board with all the suspects circled. The evidence had grown more complicated, with red lines crisscrossing between the photos of Paul Grant, Daniel Harding, Jessica, and the other people involved in her life.

"Who did Paul call?" Sara asked Jill once she was seated with her coffee in her hand.

"It took a while for one of the tech officers to make a connection. It bounced between multiple locations, but the source number leads back to Ethan Clarke."

Carla's eyes widened. "Ethan? The junior associate from Jessica's firm?"

A cold chill ran the length of Sara's spine. Her eyes narrowed as she recapped her initial assessment of Ethan after their first meeting. At first glance, he seemed enthusiastic yet harmless, a young lawyer who had been dismissed by Jessica. But the revelation that he appeared to be more involved than they had initially realised floored Sara.

It was Carla's turn to begin pacing. She eyed the whiteboard and shook her head. "What's his connection to all of this? He didn't strike me as being the type to run a criminal enterprise."

Sara got to her feet, taking her mug with her. She studied the board again, for the second time in as many minutes. Her mind darted down several rabbit warrens, searching for answers. "Ethan was close to Jessica, but she pushed him away after he made mistakes in one of her cases, the Oliver Sharpe case, to be precise. Maybe that was the start of it. Perhaps someone figured he would be easy to corrupt, recognised his ambition and desperation. He could've been roped into the money laundering scheme as a way to prove himself."

"But why would Paul call him at the warehouse?" Carla asked, frowning. "If Paul was part of this, too, why didn't he just go to whoever's running the whole thing?"

"There's a possibility that Ethan's more important than we think he is," Sara said slowly. "Or maybe... Paul felt panicked and went to the only person he thought he could still control."

"We need to talk to him," Carla said. She put her mug down on the desk beside her and moved towards the door. "If... or should I say, now that we know Ethan's involved, he might lead us to whoever's pulling the strings."

"Wait. Let's not get ahead of ourselves here. We need to be prepared for every eventuality. If we turn up unprepared and show our hand, he's likely to go on the run."

"I agree. Where do we start?"

Sara raised a finger. "Getting off the subject slightly... Jill, any news on a safe house for Jessica?"

"I keep pushing for it, boss. I haven't heard back from Rick in a while. I'll give him another call now."

Sara mulled over what other loose ends they should be tackling while Jill made the call. Jill nodded and punched the air.

"Where?" Sara mouthed.

"You're brilliant. I owe you a drink, Rick." Jill laughed and ended the call.

"He's got a house that has just become vacant out in Breinton. He's organising the cleaners to go in to give it a spruce-up. He reckons it should be ready by five this afternoon."

"Wow, that's better news than I expected to hear. At least one thing has gone in our favour in the last few hours. Right, that's given me the impetus to ruffle some feathers. Are you ready?"

Carla rolled her eyes. "I'll have to think about that."

Sara and Carla entered the reception area of the solicitors' office.

Sara flashed her ID. "We're here to see Ethan. Don't worry, we know the way."

"Hey, you can't go in there. He has a client with him," the receptionist shouted after them.

"Another lie, no doubt," Sara muttered.

She opened the door to Ethan's office; he was sitting behind his desk, alone. He quickly stood and straightened his tie nervously. But just like that, his demeanour changed.

"Inspector Ramsey," he said, his voice the epitome of calm. "Is everything all right?"

Sara didn't waste time with pleasantries. "We need to ask you a few questions, Ethan. About your colleagues, Jessica Harding and Paul Grant."

The colour in his cheeks faded at the mention of their names, and he hesitated before nodding. "Of course. What's this about?"

Sara stepped closer, her gaze locked on his. "We know."

"Sorry? Am I supposed to understand what you're talking about?"

"Don't mess with me, Ethan. Paul called you just before we arrested him. You're involved in something much bigger than you're letting on, and we're going to find out what it is. Why don't you stop wasting your time—and ours—and just tell us?"

Ethan shifted his feet and swallowed hard, his eyes flitting between Sara and Carla. "Forgive my ignorance, Inspector. I'm at a loss to know what you're talking about. Paul and I... we work together, yes, but you're wrong. I haven't spoken to him recently."

Sara crossed her arms and tapped her foot. She had trouble keeping the annoyance out of her tone. "We've traced the call, Ethan. We know Paul reached out to you when everything started to fall apart. He was seeking your help to get him out of a sticky situation. What was your role in all of this? The money laundering? The threats against Jessica?"

Ethan's façade crumbled. He sank into his chair, his hands shaking. "I didn't... I didn't want to get involved. Please, you have to believe me. I just wanted to prove myself. But Paul... he, well, he sucked me in."

Sara's eyes narrowed. "How did he include you?"

He shook his head and ran a hand around the back of his neck. "My involvement was nothing special to begin with. I played a minor role. At first, I was instructed to help with some paperwork—transferring funds between accounts and signing off on documents that I thought were legitimate. It didn't take me long to realise what was really happening. Paul was laundering money for powerful people. People with connections."

"Who are these people?" Carla asked, leaning forward. "Give us their names."

From the way his gaze darted around the room, Sara could tell that panic had set in.

"I don't know all of them. Paul was cautious. He was careful to only tell me what I needed to know. But there was one man... someone higher up. A businessman called Victor Kline. He runs a real estate empire—on the surface—but he's involved up to his neck in a lot of deals, shady ones at that."

Sara and Carla exchanged glances. Sara had heard of Victor Kline. He was a wealthy businessman with an exemplary reputation. Nonetheless, his name had been linked to several investigations over time, but nothing could ever be substantiated.

"Kline's behind the money laundering?" Sara asked.

Ethan nodded frantically. "Yes. He's been using the firm to move his money around, hiding it in offshore accounts. All of it happened through Paul. He was Kline's guy on the inside, but when Jessica started digging into things, they both panicked. They thought if she exposed the affair and the pregnancy, it would unravel everything. There was only one thing left for them to do... kidnap her."

"And you were part of it," Sara said, her voice icy cold. "You helped them, opened the door so to speak, allowing them to target her."

Ethan's face crumpled. "It's not what I wanted. I swear it wasn't. I tried to warn Jessica, but it was too late. She didn't want to listen, not after what happened with the Sharpe case. I admit that I was guilty of taking my eye off the ball with that case, only because of what was going on beneath the surface. It was a lot to get my head around."

"What do you mean, it was too late?" Carla asked.

"Paul had already set everything in motion. And now, if they know I'm talking to you, they'll come after me, too."

Sara realised the truth behind his words. Victor Kline—a man with deep pockets and even deeper connections—was the mastermind behind the entire operation. He had used Paul Grant to launder money and persuaded him to eliminate anyone who got in the way, including Jessica. And now Ethan was caught in the middle, terrified of what Kline's people would do to him if they found out he had spoken to the police. At this stage, her options were limited. At the forefront of her mind, though, she knew he was still a guilty party and should be punished for the part he'd played in Jessica's abduction.

"You should come with us. We'll take you to the station for your protection," she told him firmly, pulling out her handcuffs. "If you cooperate, we can work something out. But we're going to need your help to bring Kline down."

Ethan didn't resist, and his shoulders slumped in defeat. Sara moved behind the desk and slapped the cuffs on his wrists.

They escorted him out of the office, past the gobsmacked receptionist, who instantly reached for her phone. Outside, they crossed the road. Sara was already thinking ahead. Victor Kline had a lot of influence within the city—taking him down would be far from easy. On the bright side, they now had something that had evaded them over the years: a direct link to the mastermind behind untold corruption in the area.

Back at the station, they placed Ethan in a secure room. As Sara gathered her team, the enormity of what they were facing began to sink in.

"This goes deeper than we thought," Carla murmured. "Victor Kline's got connections all over the county, probably the country as well, for all we know. If we go after him, we need to be sure. Otherwise, he's likely to rip us apart, or get one of his contacts in authority to do it for him."

Sara nodded, her mind already turning to what their next step should be. "We'll need to bring in financial experts, get them to dig into Kline's accounts. But to do that, we're going to need to request a warrant to search his offices. If we can trace the money back to him, we'll have enough to take him down."

"We've been here before, it's a big *if*. And what about Jessica?" Carla glanced over her shoulder at Sara. "She's still a target."

"I've got every intention of sticking to my word. She'll remain in protective custody until Kline and his cohorts are banged up."

Sara was no fool. As they prepared to move forward with the case, she was all too aware that the hardest part was yet to come. Taking down someone as renowned as Victor Kline wouldn't be easy—and there was always the risk that someone on the inside was working against them; something that Sara had suspected over the years when Kline had been linked to an investigation.

But for now, they had a lead, and that lead was the first step towards bringing down the entire operation, however large it turned out to be.

12

B efore she knew it, the sun was setting, casting long shadows across the Hereford police station as Sara addressed the team in the incident room. The weight of what they had just uncovered hung heavily over them, but there was no time to waste. They would be going up against someone far more powerful than anyone they'd encountered so far—Victor Kline, a millionaire entrepreneur who, on the outside, had a spotless public image and the obvious resources to bury his secrets. *If this is what money brings with it, you can shove it up your arse.*

"All right, peeps, listen up." Sara pointed at the man's name, which she had highlighted on the whiteboard. "Victor Kline is our prime suspect. He's been using Paul Grant and other solicitors at the firm to launder money through what we're led to believe are offshore accounts. We're presuming that when Jessica Harding got too close, they decided to shut her up. As you're aware, we've already arrested Paul Grant and Ethan Clarke, but Kline is our ultimate target."

"We can't emphasise enough how thorough we need to be," Carla said. She moved to stand beside Sara and added, "Kline's a high-profile figure with powerful connections. If we're going after him, our task involves finding enough evidence to make it stick. Pure evidence, no ifs or maybes, so dig deep, folks."

Sara admired Carla's newfound confidence. She stood and smiled at her partner.

The rest of the team all nodded, their expressions serious as they absorbed the gravity of the situation. Kline was the biggest fish of all, and if they were going to bring him down, it had to be done right.

"Jessica is still downstairs, out of harm's way," Sara continued, "she'll be moved to a safe house soon. Barry, I'd like you and Craig to oversee that for me. She's our key witness, but she also remains Kline's prime target. We need to ensure her safety at all costs. No one goes near her unless I clear it first."

Sara turned to the man on her right, Lee, a member of the tech team who she'd brought in specifically to assist them at the request of DCI Price. "Start digging into Kline's accounts. We need every financial document we can get—offshore accounts, shell companies, anything that ties him to the laundering scheme. We want anything and everything you can get your hands on while we try to obtain the search warrants for his office and his home. Let's hope they don't drag their feet to give us one."

The team dispersed. Sara invited Carla into her office. They sat on either side of the desk, and Sara exhaled a large breath.

"Let's hope we can pull this off. By the way, I'm loving your new confidence out there and during the interviews we've held recently. Where has that come from?"

Carla shrugged. "I wish I knew. I suppose this case is different from any we've dealt with in the past. I think we both understand the necessity to be on our game. What did the chief have to say about it all?"

"To say she was shell-shocked would be an understatement. At first, she appeared gravely concerned, but it didn't take her long to realise that she had the A-Team on the case." Sara chuckled. "No, in all seriousness, Price agreed with the plan I put before her but also issued a warning for us to make this airtight before we face Kline with the evidence."

"Yep, I couldn't agree more. What do you really think lies ahead of us, Sara?" Carla leaned back in her chair, looking thoughtful. "Kline's going to fight this. He's probably already planning his next move, if he's aware that we've picked up Ethan."

Sara nodded, her jaw tight. "Oh yes, one thing couldn't be more certain in this life. He knows we're coming for him. He'll be prepared. But we have the upper hand—Jessica's testimony and the files she's given us were enough for us to request a search warrant. We need that to come through quickly, before Kline has a chance to cover his tracks."

Carla glanced at the clock. "I'm sensing the need to obtain that warrant quicker than we have in the past—tonight, if possible. If we wait, he could move everything offshore or shut down his shell companies before we have a chance to get our hands on him."

Sara stood, her mind made up. "Let's go see the judge."

LATER THAT AFTERNOON, Sara and Carla arrived at the home of Judge Reynolds, a no-nonsense magistrate known for being fair but tough. Upon their arrival at her detached, gated home, out in the country-side, Sara handed her the file Jessica had given them in an attempt to win her over. She had no idea if she was doing the right thing coming here. It was possible that Reynolds was involved in the scheme, although Sara doubted it from what she knew about the woman. Sara emphasised the urgency to obtain both warrants they needed to raid Victor Kline's offices and seize the financial records that would hope-fully bring his empire crashing down.

Judge Reynolds, a sharp-eyed woman in her sixties, sat behind her desk, reading through the stack of papers they had brought. The room was silent except for the soft rustle of pages being turned.

"This is quite a case you've built, Inspector," the judge said, glancing up at them. "As you know, Kline's name has come across my desk before, but nothing has ever stuck."

"That could all change this time, Judge Reynolds. We believe we have enough evidence to throw the book at him," Sara said, her voice steady. "I know he's slipped through the net a few times in the past, but I have high hopes that our luck is about to change on this one. It's all adding up to be more than solid... this time around. Jessica Harding's testimony, the financial records we've recovered from her home, and the connections to Paul Grant's laundering operation—from what we can tell, all of it leads back to one man: Kline. But we need to move quickly before he gets wind of it."

Judge Reynolds studied them for a moment before nodding. "Your coming here, at this time of night, would ordinarily put my back up." She raised a finger when Sara opened her mouth to object. "However, I can understand your urgency to bring this dreadful man down. We've met at several important functions over the years, events where he's thrown his money around and had people eating out of his hand in the process." She shuddered. "He's always given me the creeps. I'll grant you the warrant. But I also feel the need to warn you to be careful. Men like Kline don't go down without a fight."

Sara felt Carla's gaze on her. They both nodded and said in unison, "We know."

Relief flooded through Sara as Judge Reynolds picked up her pen and signed the documents. They finally had what they needed to go after Kline, but this was only the beginning. The real battle was about to start.

After thanking the judge, they returned to the station to learn that Barry and Craig had taken Jessica to the safe house.

Sara checked in with them. "Barry, it's me. Are you there yet?"

"We've been here five minutes, boss. Craig and I are giving the place the once-over."

"How's Jessica? I was hoping to see her before you left."

"Sorry."

"Don't apologise. It was important for us to visit the judge to get the warrants."

"And have you?"

"Yes. We'll make plans to hit both properties at the same time in the morning. Sorry, how's Jessica?"

"She seems fine, very quiet. But I suppose that's to be expected in the circumstances. Are you sure you don't want either Craig or me to stay with her?"

"No, I think she'll be fine. That place has never had any issues due to lack of security before, from what I can tell."

"Very well. We'll finish getting her settled and return to base."

"Tell her I'm thinking of her. Damn, I forgot to give her one of my cards. Can you write my number down and give it to her?"

"Leave it with me."

"Good man." Sara ended the call and rubbed the back of her neck. She eased her head to the right, then to the left, and it clicked several times.

She checked in with Lee to see if he'd discovered any further evidence against Kline.

He smiled and nodded. "A few bits, minor in comparison to what we're after, but I sense I'm getting close."

Sara patted him on the shoulder. "Don't stress too much about it tonight. With the warrants in hand, your skills will be needed more tomorrow. We're about to call it a day, anyway."

"Suits me, although I would be willing to work longer tonight if you need me to."

"It's fine. Can you come in early in the morning? I want to hit the ground running at around eight. I'll call a meeting to go over a plan of action, which I need to come up with at home tonight."

He nodded again. "I'm up for it. Eager to bring the bastard down, ma'am."

"Aren't we all?" she said and gave him another pat on the shoulder.

Sara drove home, her body weary but her mind still bouncing.

Luckily, Mark had called during the drive home, informing her that he would be home late and that she should not bother cooking for him. She was surprised to hear that. However, she welcomed the news because it would allow her to fix herself something quick to eat, giving her the extra time she needed to formulate a plan for the morning.

When she entered the house, she was greeted by Misty, who wrapped around her legs as she tried to remove her shoes. Defeated, she swept her cat up into her arms and kissed the top of her head. "Hey, Munchkin, have you had a good day? I bet you're hungry, aren't you?" Sara kicked off her shoes and walked through to the kitchen. She opened the back door, and Misty trotted out. She returned a few minutes later. By that time, Sara had replenished her bowls of water and food. Then she turned her attention to cooking her dinner. She placed a potato in the microwave for five minutes and grated some cheese. When the potato was cooked, she popped it in the air fryer to crisp up for another ten minutes, then opened a tin of baked beans. With everything prepared, she searched for her notebook and pen and jotted down a few notes until the ding sounded on the air fryer.

She sat at the table and ate her meal. At the same time, she continued to write. It wasn't long before the need to get everything down on paper consumed her and her dinner went cold. Sara pushed it away and flicked over another page.

Mark found her still sitting at the kitchen table, deep in thought, two hours later. He had a steaming packet of food in his hand. He kissed her and withdrew a plate from the cupboard. "You haven't eaten your meal. Was something wrong with it?"

"No, I got caught up in work. I'm fine, don't worry about me. Did you stop off at the chippy on the way home?"

"There's nothing wrong with your detective skills. Do you want to share it with me? I'm not that hungry. I don't know why I ordered it. Habit, I suppose."

"I'll pinch a few of your chips if you're offering. Did you have an emergency to attend to?"

"Yes. Something that could have easily been avoided. Makes my blood boil when parents leave their kids unsupervised with a tiny puppy."

Sara cringed. "Oh God, do I really want to hear this?"

"Poor pup was dropped by a child of five. Puppies don't bounce, and their bones are fragile. Two broken legs and now he has a permanent dent in his skull, all because the parents couldn't be bothered to supervise their child."

Sara looked up with tears in her eyes. "How awful. Some people don't deserve dogs. Can you report the owners?"

"What would be the point? They did the right thing by bringing the dog to me. Not sure if they're going to find the funds to pay for my bill, though."

"What? They can't expect you to fix their puppy for free."

He raised his eyebrow. "Can't they? I might be doing them an injustice. I'll see what happens tomorrow. I'm praying the puppy survives the night. I dread to think how the parents are going to act if he doesn't."

"Shit. Hey, if you need any assistance, make sure you call the station."

"What? Can't I call you directly?"

Sara chewed her lip. "Usually, I would offer to be on call, you know that, but we've got a raid planned for the morning."

"A raid?" He seemed puzzled.

Sara loosely explained the situation without mentioning names or going over the nitty-gritty details they had uncovered.

"Wow! It sounds dangerous. You will take care, won't you?"

"Don't worry, that goes without saying. I intend to take plenty of backup with us."

"Good. Are you finished making notes now?"

She slid her notebook aside, sensing that Mark had something on his mind. "I'm all yours. Is there something you want to discuss?"

"Yes and no. What I really want to do is apologise to you for being such a grouch lately." He reached for her hand and kissed it.

"Why don't we pour ourselves a glass of wine and go through to the lounge?"

Mark nodded. "Can you get the wine while I start on my takeaway?"

"Go for it." She watched him leave the room and collected the glasses and bottle of wine from the fridge.

Mark was tucking into his fish and chips and glanced sideways at her when she sat next to him on the sofa. He chinked his glass against hers. "To us."

"To us. There's never a need to apologise, not when you've been through so much. I'm just glad you're back on track again."

"I am, sort of. I had a lull between patients today, and I got to thinking... about us. I felt sad because of the way I've treated you over the last few months. All you were doing was trying to help me, and the number of times I've snapped your head off..." He leaned over and kissed her with his greasy lips. "Oops, sorry. I love you. Can you ever forgive me?"

She wagged her finger. "There's nothing to forgive. That's what true love is... never having to say sorry."

"You're adorable, one of the nicest people ever to walk this earth, Sara. I don't deserve you."

"Nonsense. If we're being open with each other, I have been a bit put out, only because I've felt you were shutting me out."

He bowed his head. "I was. Bloody-minded as ever. I felt it was my problem to solve. I was wrong. I want to put that right."

She frowned. "You don't have to do that."

"I do. I want to book a holiday for us; it needn't be until the spring. Let's face it, we haven't been away for months."

Sara contemplated the idea. She'd like nothing more than to spend time on a beach with him, sipping margaritas. Maybe she'd have the headspace to turn her attention to their future, once the current investigation was done and dusted. "I think you're right. It would be wonderful for us to get away. Can we discuss it further at the weekend?"

"Of course. I'm glad we're back on the same page, at last."

"I don't think we veered off course that much. Your treatment probably made things seem a thousand times worse."

"You're right, as usual."

Sara helped Mark finish his supper, and then they had an early night. In bed, they held each other tightly, but Mark stopped short of going to the next stage. Which was fine with Sara. He was worth waiting for.

13

———

The following morning, Sara rose early, at five-thirty. She went downstairs to make yet more notes about the plan she needed to put into action that morning. She jotted down the key elements that would need to take place and the different teams she would need to assemble before the raid could happen.

Mark found her an hour later, busy scribbling at the kitchen table. "I thought you'd be doing this. You should have said if you wanted to continue with the task last night, our chat could have waited."

She raised her head for a kiss. He willingly obliged. "No, it couldn't. I needed to spend time with you."

"Ditto. I've got an early start. I'll be worried about you all day. Can you find time in your busy schedule today to let me know you're okay?"

She smiled. "I promise. I'll be surrounded by professionals. Try not to worry, darling."

"Easier said than done. Luckily, I have a full diary ahead of me today. Love you." He kissed her and left without having any breakfast.

Sara rolled her eyes and said to Misty, "He's nuts. I doubt if he's even realised."

She completed her notes and raced upstairs to have a shower and get ready. Then she fed Misty and set off at seven-thirty.

Sara was pleased to see quite a few cars belonging to the rest of her team already parked outside the station.

"Morning, ma'am," Jeff said as soon as she entered the reception area. "The briefing room is a hive of activity this morning. Don't forget to let me know if I can be of assistance."

"I will. If you can arrange cover, why don't you join us?"

"I'll do that. Thank you."

Sara nodded and punched her number into the keypad, and the door sprang open. She turned right, towards the briefing room. "Morning, Carla. How are you?"

"I'm all right, I think. My mind was racing last night. I don't suppose I was alone."

"You weren't." Sara withdrew her notebook from her handbag and flipped through the dozens of pages of notes she had made at home during her two stints.

"Do you think we're ready for this?" Carla asked as more officers filed into the briefing room.

"We have to be," Sara replied. "This is our one shot to take Kline down. If we miss something or give him time to cover his tracks, we'll lose him. Knowing his type, he'll probably have a private jet on standby, ready to leave the country."

Carla nodded, her eyes narrowing. "More than likely. I just hope Jessica will be safe this time. Kline might still have people out there—people who'd do anything to silence her."

Sara's expression hardened. "I have no intention of letting that happen. I've decided to send a team out there to be with her."

THE MEETING BEGAN, and everyone remained attentive for the next fifteen minutes.

At the end of it, Sara asked, "Is everything clear? Are there any questions?" The room remained silent. Sara added, "What I really wanted to do was hit Kline's home and office at the same time. It has since come to my attention that he has three properties he uses throughout Hereford. We're going to need to get two further warrants before we can hit his personal properties. Until then, we need to focus all our attention on the office, instead." She tried not to let her enthusiasm slip, but it was difficult, knowing that once they showed up at his office, Kline was likely to set out to give them the slip. Or worse. She shrugged the sense of doom off. They were ready to rumble, to make the best of the situation. Her mood improved slightly when she received a text message from the team she had dispatched to watch over Jessica.

ALL CLEAR. **Jessica is safe and secure.**

SARA FELT a small surge of relief. For now, Jessica was out of harm's way. She knew how quickly the situation could change if Kline realised how close they were to bringing him down.

"Let's move out," Sara said.

Everyone filed out of the room.

Carla pulled her back. "Are you all right? You seem on edge."

"Wouldn't you be?" Sara snapped and then tutted. "Sorry, that was uncalled for. If we screw this up…"

"We won't, as long as we remain positive. I can't even imagine what it must be like to be in your shoes right now, with the amount of responsibility sitting on your shoulders. But I want to tell you that you're not alone. You've got a lot of professional and willing people behind you. I'm certain they won't let you down."

Sara smiled and pointed at the door. "We need to go, and thanks, Carla. I needed that boost."

They left the station and led the convoy of cars to the location.

The raid on Victor Kline's offices went smoother than expected. The element of surprise worked in their favour, and the teams moved quickly through the sleek, glass-walled building, securing files, computers and financial records. Kline's staff appeared shocked as the police swept through the offices, gathering everything they thought was relevant.

Sara and Carla searched through the rooms with one purpose: to find Kline's private office. Sara had asked the receptionist and other staff members where it was. All of them had glared at her and refused to open their mouths. Carla had discovered a secret panel in the hallway which led them up to the top floor of the building, only for them to find the door was locked. Sara returned to the reception area and demanded the key.

"I can't give it to you because I don't have it. No one is allowed up there, not even Kline's secretary," the receptionist said.

"Fair enough. We'll break it down." Sara returned upstairs, accompanied by an officer. "I need to break it down."

"I can sort that for you, ma'am. I'll get the equipment from the car." He came back moments later with an enforcer in hand.

Sara beamed. "That should do the trick."

"We'll see."

Sara and Carla turned their heads away as he aimed a blow at the door. It took a couple of attempts until the officer broke through. Sara entered the room and scanned the area. Kline's office was as polished as his public image: minimalist, expensive, and utterly devoid of anything personal. The man himself, however, was nowhere to be seen.

"Where is he?" Carla muttered, scanning their surroundings.

Another officer entered the room and informed them, "We've conducted a thorough search of the premises. Kline's not in the building. His secretary said he was supposed to be in this morning, but he hasn't shown up."

Sara's stomach tightened. She kicked out at a chair with enough force to send it hurtling across the room. If he'd been here, he would have been in his office. Kline had slipped away. The question was, had he been tipped off? Did he know they were coming?

"We'll find him," Sara said, her voice firm, the urgency clear. "Forget about him for now. Start going through the files. Everything we need is here. Tell the men to keep their eyes open for more secret passageways."

Sara and Carla began to search Kline's personal office. They had to break into the drawers in his desk. They boxed up all the paperwork, whether it was significant or not. Sara's phone rang. It was the officer assigned to Jessica's protective detail. She answered the call, a sense of dread looming over her. She put it on speaker so Carla could hear.

"Inspector Ramsey?" The officer's voice was shaky.

"What's going on?" Sara demanded, her fear escalating.

"It's Jessica," the officer said. He paused and sucked in a breath. "She's gone. Someone took her."

His words knocked the air out of her lungs. "What do you mean, she's gone? How could she just vanish?"

"We don't know. There was no sign of a struggle, but the house was empty when we did our last check. Whoever took her knew what they were doing. We were watching the front. They must have gained access from the back. When we checked, there was a lane at the rear of the property. We should have been more thorough. All I can do is offer you an apology."

Sara's hand tightened around the phone, and she shook her head, trying to dislodge the one fact that was prominent in her mind: Kline had taken Jessica. Somehow, despite their best efforts, he had found her and now he had her in his grasp.

"We're going to find her," Carla said, determined.

Sara's heart pounded as she tried to focus. Victor Kline had Jessica, and now everything they had worked for was on the line. It was no longer just about taking down a criminal empire—it was about saving Jessica's life... again!

And the clock was ticking.

14

"No!" Sara screamed. "This can't be happening. Not again." She ended the call and could barely feel her legs as she rushed down the hallway, her mind clouded with a mix of fear and urgency. *The bastard has been one step ahead of us all this time.*

Jessica was gone, taken either by Victor Kline or by someone working for him. Sara was furious. She couldn't help feeling let down. She did her best to set that aside for now. Her disappointment was soon replaced by anger. She stopped running and bashed her fists on the wall. After all they'd done to protect her, it still hadn't been enough. "I'm guilty of taking my eye off the ball. All this is my fault. I was so intent on getting Kline that I forgot to weigh up the options of what might happen if we failed."

Carla stopped beside her and grasped her arms. She turned Sara around to face her. "You've got to stop thinking that way, Sara. Neither of us could have imagined what was likely to happen. As far as we knew, Jessica was in a safe house. You did all you could to protect her. It also means—and believe me, I hate to say this—that we've got a mole in the station. Someone in that meeting today must be on Kline's payroll."

"Yet another issue we need to deal with, as well as finding Jessica again. The poor woman must be scared shitless. We've let her down, Carla. Correction, I have."

Carla's expression never altered; it was still set in grim determination, a stark contrast to what Sara was feeling. "Stop blaming yourself, Sara. What we need to figure out is how the hell they got to her. Who is feeding Kline the information?"

"I don't know," Sara replied, her mind racing. "But we need to find out fast. We've opened the investigation up and brought in outsiders, only for it to smack us in the face. I'm not sure who we can trust any more. One thing is certain, though: if Kline does have her, there's every possibility he'll kill her rather than take the risk of her escaping or us rescuing her. Either way, I suspect we haven't got much time to find her."

"Should we inform Daniel? We've kept him out of the loop so far."

"At Jessica's request. I think we should keep it that way, for now. I'll take the flack, if any comes our way. At this stage, as I've already stated, we don't know who we can trust. Let's finish up here and get back to the station."

"I have something to add, but you're not going to like it."

Sara said, "Go on, hit me with it."

"All this paperwork we're collecting. What if the mole is with us now? What if they are overseeing our mission with the intention of concealing the papers?"

Sara covered her face with her hands and growled. "You're right. Get our team together, now." They sought out Barry, Craig and Marissa and pulled them to one side. Sara closed the door to the empty office they were in and ran through what had happened.

"Shit!" Barry said. "We should have been at the house, protecting her. The bastards wouldn't have got past me and Craig."

Sara raised a hand. "There's no point saying or thinking that, Barry, what's done is done. The reason we've called you together is to tell you to keep your eyes open. There are six other officers here with us today. There's a possibility that one of them is a mole."

The three team members all shook their heads, dumbfounded by the discouraging news.

"When we leave here, I'm going to have a word with the chief. Tell her in no uncertain terms that we're going to handle the rest of the case ourselves. While it's been nice having the extra hands during the investigation, look where it has got us. Carla raised a good point, which is why we've called you together. If the mole is here, it means they're likely to tamper with the evidence, either try to hide it or even destroy it. That's what I want you to watch out for. I need you to keep your eyes and ears open. If you notice anything suspicious, report back to me immediately. I'm going to get in touch with the station and ask Jeff to send a van out here; we're going to need to transport everything back to base. If the mole cottons on to what we're up to, there's every chance they'll panic. Keep vigilant, that's all we can do for now."

"Will do, boss. We won't let you down," Barry assured her.

Sara smiled and slapped him on the back. "You guys never let me down. I regret putting us in this position. I wanted you to know how much I trust you."

"We know you do, boss," Marissa added.

Sara nodded and clapped her hands. "Right, let's get back out there. Watch and listen."

The three team members left the room, and Sara placed the call to the station. There was one more person she felt she could trust: the desk sergeant. She rang him and filled him in on what was happening. He was shocked to learn the truth and promised that he would keep his eyes open.

The van arrived within half an hour. It was down to Sara and Carla to oversee the loading of the vehicle. Once the task was completed, she called her team together once more.

"Anything?" she asked them.

They all shook their heads.

"Nothing obvious from what we could tell, boss."

It wasn't the news Sara wanted to hear. "Okay, keep alert at the other end. Barry, can you and Craig oversee the unloading and ensure that every box is taken to the secure room at the station? Marissa, you can join Carla and me in the incident room. We'll thrash out where we turn next."

Back at the station, Sara dismissed the rest of the team. She congratulated them on a job well done, not giving anything away about Jessica's abduction. She scrutinised the crowd of men before her, searching for any chinks in their behaviour that might alert her to who the mole was. Unfortunately, the person proved to be craftier than she'd anticipated.

Frustrated, Sara and Carla returned to the incident room, where they brought Jill up to date on the events that had occurred while they were out.

"Oh shit! I hope he doesn't harm her," Jill said. "Do you want me to do some digging, boss? Check out the records of all the officers involved in the operation?"

Sara winked at her. "You read my mind. The slightest dubious action that shows up, I want to hear about it ASAP, Jill."

She nodded, her fingers already flying across the keyboard.

Carla handed Sara a coffee. "Here, I think we're in dire need of a caffeine hit. I've made it stronger than usual."

Sara stared at her mug. "You're not kidding. Is there any milk in it?"

Carla laughed. "Yep. I told you it was strong."

Sara carried her mug over to the whiteboard, and her gaze fixed on Kline's name. This wasn't about what Kline had been up to any more. It was personal. Jessica's life was in danger, for the second time in as many days. She shook her head in disbelief.

"I can sense you're intent on blaming yourself again. Stop it, Sara, it's not going to do any good. Umm... shouldn't you tell Price what's going on?"

Sara's gaze left the board and rose to the ceiling. "You're right. I'll go now. I might get a decent cup of coffee there."

"There's an answer to that. Make your own next time." Carla

grinned and added, "I'll help Jill. It's not in me to sit here, doing nothing."

"Good idea. I won't be too long, I hope. She's going to be livid when she hears the truth."

Sara's assumption proved to be right. Carol Price flung her pen across the other side of the room when Sara told her that Jessica had been abducted again.

"How could this happen? She was in a safe house. At least that's what you told me you were arranging for her."

"She was."

"I repeat, so how was this allowed to happen?"

Sara shrugged. "It was out of my hands, boss. It would appear that we have a mole on the case, leaking information to Kline and his men."

"A mole? Do you know who? It's not a member of your team, surely, is it?"

"Not my immediate team. I'd put my life on that. But someone else we've been working closely with lately. Jill and Carla are going through the officers' files now to see if they can find the culprit."

Carol Price closed her eyes and let out a deep sigh. "I never thought I'd live to see this day. I've always worked hard to keep my ship steady. Corruption was rife around here at one point, before Kline's day. I thought those days were long behind us."

"Clearly not, boss. Don't worry, we'll find out who it is. At the moment, I find myself in a dilemma about whether or not to go after Kline today. What if he senses we're closing in on him and decides to kill Jessica? I won't be able to forgive myself."

"While I can understand your apprehension, Sara, you're going to have to set that aside for now and do what is best for Jessica."

"Any advice you have to offer will be gratefully received. I'm not ashamed to admit that I feel like I'm drowning right now, although I would never share that with my team."

Carol wagged her finger like a metronome. "Don't give me that bullshit. You're one of the strongest women I know. You can do this;

you've hit a bump in the road. It's not insurmountable. You've over-come worse throughout your career."

Sara pulled a face. "I have? I can't for the life of me think what that might be."

"Nonsense. All you're doing is putting obstacles in the way. Have you spoken to Judge Reynolds about the extra warrants you need?"

"No, not yet. I'll get on that when I leave here. Thanks for keeping faith with me."

"I'd be foolish not to. Now get out of here. Shoulders back and march on, the way we always do. You've got this, Sara. Stop doubting yourself and stop allowing this man's reputation to dominate your thoughts."

"You're right. I think that's what is behind the doubts running through my mind. The clout he must have behind him. We have no idea where this investigation is going to lead us."

"You've got a weapon of your own at your disposal that you're forgetting about."

Sara frowned and tilted her head. "I have?"

"Judge Reynolds. From what you've told me, she's been trying to cast the net over Kline for years. With her behind you, there should be no stopping you. Now, stop all this talk of doubts weighing you down and get on with it. Bring him in, let him sweat it out in a cell for a while. I can guarantee the cracks will begin to show before long."

"Thanks for the kick up the arse, boss."

Price smiled. "Feel free to drop by for one of those weekly, if you think it will help."

Sara laughed and left, disappointed that she hadn't been offered a decent cup of coffee. She headed back to the incident room but made a pit stop at the ladies' on the way.

When she entered the incident room, she found Jill and Carla deep in conversation. She approached them and asked, "Any news?"

"We think we've found a tenuous link."

Sara peered over Jill's shoulder and looked at the screen. "We searched through everyone's Facebook accounts, and Constable John Wheaton is friends with Ethan Clarke."

"I don't know him, do you?"

Jill and Carla both shook their heads.

Sara rang Barry. "Can you talk? Move to somewhere you won't be overheard."

"Doing it now. Okay, I'm free to talk, boss."

"Do you know Constable John Wheaton?"

"I've known him for a few years, but only to say hello to. Can I ask why?"

"We've discovered a connection between him and Ethan Clarke."

"Damn. I'm watching him now. I hadn't noticed it before, but he's got a bit of a sweat on and his eyes are everywhere. What do you want me to do?"

"Keep an eye on him. We're going to need to catch him in the act, just to make things watertight."

"I'm on it, boss. Don't worry."

"Good man." Sara ended the call. "Barry told me that Wheaton is in the secure room, acting suspiciously. He's going to keep a close eye on him."

"What about the team who were sent to the safe house?" Carla asked. "When we put someone in the safe house, it's supposed to be privileged information. How did Wheaton find out where Jess was?"

Sara nodded. Her partner had made a valid point. She ran a hand through her hair. "I need to bring Jeff into this. I know I can trust him."

Carla agreed. "I would, the sooner the better. Before it's too late and—"

Sara raised a hand. "Please don't finish your sentence. Right now, we need to focus on where they might have taken her."

They studied the map Carla had laid out on the desk beside her, searching for a possible location. "Kline's network is vast, and his resources could take Jessica anywhere. We're aware of his property empire in and around Hereford, but we mustn't forget that there are also industrial locations and warehouses linked to his business, as well."

"We should start with Kline's properties," Carla suggested. She circled a couple of spots on the map with a marker. "I don't think he'd risk taking her too far, not yet. Especially if he knows we're on to him."

Sara nodded. "I'm going to call Judge Reynolds, chase up the warrants. I know the team will be stretched now that I've dismissed the others. We need to hit these locations simultaneously. Kline's smart, but if we act fast, we might catch him before he moves her again."

Lee, the tech guy, who they hadn't ditched, waved a sheet of paper to gain Sara's attention. "This might help. I've got my hands on some recent financial documents from Kline's office. I've been specifically looking for recent transactions and discovered that there's been a lot of activity in a warehouse just outside town. I dug deeper and found that it's registered to one of his shell companies."

"That could be it," Sara said, her eyes narrowing. "If he's still nearby, it's the perfect place to keep her." Sara didn't hesitate. "We're going there. I'll nip downstairs and see where the land lies with Wheaton. I'll have a word with Jeff at the same time. In the meantime, Lee, can you organise a drone?"

"That's a great idea. I also wanted to point out that the warehouse is surrounded by fields, something we need to bear in mind."

"You're suggesting he might bring a helicopter in to escape," Sara said, her brow furrowed as the different scenarios rattled through her mind.

Lee gave her the thumbs-up and put his head down again, his hands flying across the keyboard.

Sara tore down the concrete staircase and into the reception area. "Can you arrange cover for ten minutes?" she asked Jeff.

"We're in luck. Tracy has just clocked on."

Sara gestured for him to join her in the room off to her right. She paced the floor until he entered. They both sat at the table, and Sara went over the details they'd found out about Wheaton.

"What the fu... he's always been a likeable kind of guy, but thinking about it, there has been a change in him recently. I tried to talk to him about it, but he put the shutters up, told me it was a personal problem that he needed to deal with himself."

"What about the men you sent out to the safe house? What can you tell me about them?"

"Matt Horlock and Kevin Dobbs." He paused to think, then nodded. "Dobbs is friendly with Wheaton, so that might be the link. You wait until I get my hands on them..."

Sara chuckled. "You're going to need to stand in line, Jeff. Barry rang me. He's in the secure room with Wheaton, watching what he gets up to. My dilemma is that we need to shake a leg, get the team together—my team, who I would trust with my life—and get out to Kline's properties. I need to chase up the warrants. I should have done that before bringing you up to date. I'll get on it now. The thing is, we're going to be stretched on personnel. Do you have anyone available who you can fully trust?"

"Yes, a couple of the older men. They're on duty now. I'll call them."

He left the room, and Sara rang the judge. She kept her fingers crossed when she made the call.

"Hello, Inspector. You've caught me between sessions. I was just about to sign the warrants. I see he has a number of them."

"He has, Judge Reynolds. Umm... there's been a further development you should know about."

"Oh, and that is?"

"Kline was behind the abduction of Jessica Harding..."

"That's right. I remember you telling me that, which has led to your request for the original warrant. There's more?"

"Yes. We took Jessica to a safe house while we dealt with Kline." She paused to replenish the breath in her lungs. "He found out about it, and we believe he's abducted her again."

"Jesus. How was this allowed to happen?"

"Again, it's pure speculation on our part at the moment, but we believe it's an inside job. We have the person under surveillance as we speak. He won't get away with it."

"I think you'll find that, between them, they already have, Inspector."

"Yes, what I should have said was..."

"I know what you meant. I'm signing the warrants now. I'll get my secretary to send them to you ASAP. Good luck. I think you're going to need it."

"We're going to have everything crossed when we raid Kline's properties. Thank you for your help."

Jeff entered the room. "All sorted. They're on their way back to the station. They should be here within ten minutes."

"Thanks, Jeff." Sara rose from her seat and patted his arm. "You're a good man. The warrants have been granted. I'm going to need to pull my men out of the secure room now. Can I leave you to deal with Wheaton? I'll check with Barry first, see what the git has been up to since I last spoke with him."

"It'll be my pleasure to deal with the little prick."

The drive to the warehouse was tense. Sara's hands gripped the steering wheel so tightly that her knuckles turned white. Carla sat beside her, scanning the roads for anything suspicious. Neither of them said much, the urgency of the situation pressing down on them.

The endless scenarios raced through Sara's mind, sweat developing on her top lip. Kline was smart. She was confident he wouldn't take any unnecessary risks, and she was also positive that he wouldn't keep Jessica in the same place for long. Finding her had to be their priority. Sara feared if they didn't locate her soon, she might disappear for good.

As if reading her mind, Carla broke the silence and said, "I'm worried, Sara. Kline's been one step ahead of us this whole time. What if... what if we're already too late?"

"We need to remain positive," Sara replied, feeling anything but herself. "We're going to find her."

Carla nodded. She stared at the road ahead, her expression grim. "I'm glad you finally relented and agreed to request an Armed Response Team to attend."

"Fingers crossed they're not needed."

They both knew the odds weren't in their favour, but their confidence needed to remain intact. They had to believe they could save her.

When they arrived, the tactical team was there, at the arranged location, on the road adjacent to where the warehouse was situated. It was a remote location that only those with specific knowledge would consider investigating. Sara exited the car and spoke with the officer in charge. She had worked with Dave Salter several times over the years. She went over the information with him, and he agreed she should lead the raid, but she was to call on him if things got hairy.

The building loomed in front of them, old and weathered but still functional. There were no signs of activity on the outside, but Sara's gut told her they were in the right place.

"We'll go in quietly, reassess once we're inside," she told the team. "There's no telling how many people Kline has in there, but we can't risk alerting them until we have a better understanding of what's going on in there."

Carla, always ready for action, checked her Taser and nodded. "Let's do this."

The team moved towards the building, their footsteps silent but purposeful. Sara and Carla led the way, creeping around the side of the warehouse, looking for a point of entry. They found a door, unlocked it and slipped inside.

The interior of the warehouse was vast and dimly lit by a few hanging bulbs. The smell of dust and oil filled the air, and the faint hum of machinery buzzed in the distance. The team spread out, searching the area, their weapons raised, ready for action.

Sara's heart pounded as they crept deeper into the building. Every step felt like a ticking clock, each second bringing them closer to finding Jessica, or losing her forever.

Carla was the first to hear it. She alerted everyone to the sound: a faint murmur coming from a room at the rear.

Sara signalled, and she moved quickly towards the source of the noise, the team following close behind. As they approached the door, Sara paused. She turned to put a finger to her lips. Voices—one of them was familiar.

Jessica.

It was enough for Sara to act upon. Without delay, she kicked the door open, Taser drawn, and rushed inside.

Her instincts proved to be right. Jessica was there, tied to a chair in the centre of the room, her face pale and bruised, but she was alive. Standing beside her, with a gun pointed at her head, was a man Sara recognised immediately.

Victor Kline.

He seemed calm, almost bored, as if he had expected them to find him. His expensive suit was rumpled, and there was a faint smile on his face as he glared at Sara.

"Right on time," Kline said, his voice smooth and mocking. "I knew you'd come."

"Kline, put the gun down," Sara ordered, her voice cold and steady, despite her insides churning. "It's over. There's an Armed Response Team outside. I only have to give them the word…"

Kline raised an eyebrow, still holding the gun against Jessica's temple. "Over? I don't think so. You've been chasing me, trying to tear down everything I've built, but you don't understand. People like me don't go to prison. We never lose."

"Let her go," Carla growled, her Taser aimed at his chest.

Kline chuckled, a low, dark sound that sent a chill through the room. "Oh, I'll let her go on one proviso."

Sara had an inkling what that would be. "Which is?"

"You let me walk out of here. I've got a helicopter waiting. I'd call that a fair exchange, wouldn't you?"

Sara quickly ran through the options open to her. They couldn't let Kline walk free. He was too dangerous, too powerful. But she didn't want to risk Jessica's life either.

Kline seemed to sense her hesitation. "You don't really have a choice," he said smoothly. "You either let me go, or she dies."

They were at a stand-off, but she wasn't willing to give up just yet. She caught Carla's eye, and a silent message passed between them.

Carla moved slightly, adjusting her stance, her eyes never leaving Kline. Sara could feel the tension intensify between her and her partner.

Then, without warning, Carla took the shot and fired her Taser.

Kline immediately dropped to the floor, his body violently jerking because of the fifty thousand volts surging through him. His gun slid across the floor towards them. Sara gestured for Barry and Craig to deal with Kline, while she and Carla checked if Jessica was okay.

Carla quickly untied Jessica, who collapsed into her arms. She was shaken up but alive.

"It's over," Carla whispered, her tone thick with relief. "You're safe."

Sara stood, breathing heavily. She looked down at Kline, who was cuffed and being dragged to his feet by her colleagues.

"You think this is over?" Kline sneered, his face twisted with anger. "You'll never get all of us. People like me don't fail."

Sara's gaze latched on to his. "I've got news for you. You already have."

Kline was led away. Sara turned to Jessica, who was still trembling but managed a small, shaky smile.

"Thank you," Jessica whispered, her voice raw with emotion. "I thought... I thought it was truly the end this time."

Sara smiled softly and rested a hand on her shoulder. "It's not over yet. But this time, you have my word. We'll make sure you're safe."

Carla nodded. "We'll take Kline down. He won't get away with it this time. We'll get all of them."

They went back to the car. Sara left Carla to settle Jessica in the back and crossed the gravel to speak with Dave.

"Sorry, you weren't needed after all. We expected him to be joined by his fearsome entourage, but he was alone. Thanks for attending, anyway."

Dave nodded and smiled. "Glad not to have been of service for a change. Our involvement usually means that things have gone too far."

They shook hands. Sara gave a thumbs-up to the rest of the team she spotted in the back of the van. The side door slid shut, and Dave jumped behind the steering wheel, then drove off.

Barry drove his car past her. Sara ducked down to see an angry Kline glaring at her in the back seat.

She walked back to the car, her legs feeling lighter than they had done all week. "We rescued her. What a relief."

15

Back at the station, the mood was both triumphant and tense. Victor Kline was in custody, his power and influence seemingly crumbling around him, but there was still a lingering sense of doubt amongst the team that the fight was far from over. Sara sat in the incident room, a celebratory mug of coffee in hand, staring at the board that had been the centre of their investigation for days. Kline's smug face, now crossed through with red marker, stared back at her from the cluster of suspects and leads.

Carla sighed heavily and sat beside her. She had with her a thick file they'd taken from Kline's office. "I thought taking Kline down would feel more satisfying," she muttered, shaking her head. "But it doesn't. Not yet."

"It will, eventually. We're far from finished. Kline may be in custody, but he's right, his network is still out there, and they will have set things in motion, prepared for this eventuality. People like him don't act alone, and they won't give up just because he's behind bars."

Carla nodded, her frustration clear. "We've only cut off one head of the snake. There's more to this than we've uncovered, and it's clear

Kline has loyal people in high places. If we don't dismantle the rest of the operation, they'll more than likely regroup, and Jessica will still be in danger. What are we going to do about her, by the way?"

"I need to have a word with Price. See if she can come up with somewhere new where we can place her. I know we've plugged the leak for now, but I don't feel as though I can trust anyone other than our team and Jeff. That's an awful thing for me to say, but it happens to be the truth."

"Hey, I'm with you on that score, one hundred percent. I think it's appalling that we're in this situation. It just shows the power Kline and his associates have and why Judge Reynolds has been trying to bring him down for years."

"That reminds me, I should give her a call and let her know that her wish has come true."

Carla frowned. "Her wish?"

"She told me she wanted to see him banged up in a cell, sooner rather than later. That's why she was so eager to sign off on the warrants."

"Ah, gotcha." Carla smiled and took a sip of her coffee.

Sara withdrew her phone from her pocket. It rang in her hand. "DI Sara Ramsey."

"It's Jeff, ma'am. Kline's solicitor has arrived."

"Thanks for letting me know. He can wait for ten minutes until I've made an important call. It's not me paying his bill, and Kline can afford the extra expense."

Jeff chuckled. "I agree. I'll pass on the message."

"I'll be down soon." Sara ended the call and immediately rang Judge Reynolds.

"This must be your lucky day, Inspector. You've caught me between cases again."

"Great. Thanks for taking my call. I'm ringing to let you know that your wish has been granted."

"What? Are you telling me that you've caught the bastard?"

"We have indeed."

"Hang on, at what cost?"

"Don't worry, Jessica Harding is safe. He had a gun to her head, literally, when we showed up at one of his warehouses. He drove a hard bargain."

"Which consisted of what?"

"He said he would release her on one proviso... that we let him go. He had a helicopter waiting on standby in a nearby field."

"Shit. How did you manage to arrest him then?"

"My partner tasered him. It was a risk, knowing he had a gun jabbed against Jessica's temple, but it paid off in the end."

"Amazing work. I'm thrilled for you and your team."

"Now all we have to do is find and arrest his associates, otherwise the nightmare will continue."

"Good luck. You know where I am if you need any warrants signed in a hurry."

"I was hoping you'd say that. I'll be in touch soon."

"I'll hold you to that, Inspector. I mean it, day or night, just holler."

"I appreciate it. Thank you, Judge."

Sara ended the call and punched the air. "It's not what you know, it's who you know that matters. Let's hope our healthy relationship continues after this investigation has ended."

Carla grinned. "Sounds like a match made in heaven."

"Right, sup up. We need to question the smug bastard." She peered at her watch. "It's eleven-thirty already. Where has the morning gone?"

"I doubt if we'll be long. I'm guessing he'll go down the 'no comment' route, like the other despots we've questioned over the years who have had a lot to lose."

Sara drank the rest of her coffee and bounced out of her chair. "There's one way to find out."

Jeff pointed out Kline's solicitor as soon as they arrived. Not that it was needed. The grey-haired man in his dapper navy-blue suit stuck out like a sore thumb in the reception area. Sara approached him and offered her hand.

He stared at it but refused to shake it. "I haven't got time for pleasantries, Inspector. I demand to speak with my client before the interview takes place."

"I'll allow you that privilege, Mr Cummings. I'll show you through to the interview room."

He rose from his seat and picked up his briefcase.

"Can you fetch Kline for us, Sergeant?"

"On my way, ma'am."

Once they had relocated, Sara asked Cummings if he'd like a drink while he waited for his client.

"I'll decline your offer. I have certain standards I like to maintain."

"Suit yourself. Take a seat. Sorry, it's not padded. We have certain standards we like to maintain, as I'm sure you'll appreciate."

Sara and Carla left the room and high-fived each other.

"You showed him, the tosser," Carla muttered.

"It was a pleasure, too."

Jeff appeared with Kline at the end of the hallway. His gaze held Sara's all the way.

"Your solicitor is waiting for you," Sara told him.

"It's about time. What was the holdup?"

"You'll have to ask Mr Cummings that." She pushed the door open and saw Cummings jump to his feet. "You have five minutes before the interview begins."

"That's not long enough," Cummings objected.

She tilted her head. "Isn't it? I think you'll find it's long enough to advise your client to issue the infamous two words, don't you?" She swiftly closed the door on any denial or further complaint Cummings was about to issue.

Again, Carla high-fived her. "You're enjoying this, aren't you?"

"Yep, a little too much, which means it's bound to come back and haunt me, eventually."

After the allocated time was up, Sara and Carla entered the room and took a seat opposite the two smartly dressed men, who both looked out of their comfort zone.

Carla started the recording and announced who was present in the room.

"Mr Kline, you're aware of the charges against you today: the abduction of a female solicitor, Jessica Harding. What do you have to say about that?"

Cummings shot his client a look. Sara could tell he hadn't been told about the incident.

Kline grinned, showing off the white teeth he'd probably paid a fortune to have straightened and whitened, and said the words she'd been expecting to hear.

"No comment. Next." He folded his arms, and his grin turned into a sickening smirk.

The rest of the interview went pretty much the same way. Thirty minutes later, Sara drew the meeting to a halt. Before she ended the recording, she issued him with a word of warning. "My team is sifting through the files we retrieved from your office now. It won't be long before we uncover the evidence we need to put you in prison... for life."

"We'll see. I mean, no comment," he replied and rubbed his hands together.

"And here's another snippet of information for you: we've also arrested the mole you planted at the station."

He shrugged and snarled, "Who gives a shit? There are plenty of bent coppers waiting in the wings to replace him."

Sara smiled and winked at him. "Thanks for admitting that for the recording. This interview is now over."

Cummings leaned in and whispered something in his ear.

His client pulled away. "Just do your frigging job and get me out of here."

Sara nodded at the constable at the back of the room. "Take him back to his cell."

Kline's eyes narrowed as he stood. "Be careful, Inspector, I'd keep an eye open at all times, if I were you."

"Is that a threat, Mr Kline?"

She and Carla left their seats.

"It's a promise. Just because I'm banged up, it doesn't mean that my operation will grind to a halt. Far from it, I assure you."

"Don't say anything else," Cummings warned.

Kline glanced his way and said, "Why not? It's the truth."

He was escorted back to his cell.

Sara faced Cummings and said, "You know the way."

"I do. You'll be hearing from me soon, Inspector."

"I'll look forward to it. Have a good day."

"Oh, I will, don't worry."

They watched him walk up the corridor.

The constable returned from the cell area and opened the door to the reception to allow Cummings to enter.

"I wasn't about to escort him back. The man gave me the bloody creeps. His sort always does," Sara said, shuddering.

"Don't let him get to you. With Kline behind bars, he'll probably be drawing dole money by the end of the year."

"Let's hope so."

They climbed the stairs to the incident room.

Carla said, "Kline will be sitting in his cell now, hoping that one of his people steps up to offer the bail money."

"I doubt if he'll be granted bail. Let's hope he goes before Judge Reynolds. That'll make her day."

"I bet she'll spend the next couple of days going through the upcoming court cases and will jump at the chance to preside over the hearing."

"It's a great achievement, having a judge of her stature on our side."

They entered the incident room, and Sara walked towards the whiteboard.

"We have his financial records, but we haven't tied all the threads together. There are still names missing. These are the individuals who have been instrumental in helping him retain his power. Let's do some more digging. Barry, can you and Craig bring some of those boxes upstairs? We'll go through them together."

A few hours later, Lee pulled up some information on the screen and announced, "I've been going through Kline's offshore accounts. I've highlighted several transactions between him and several shell companies, but I haven't managed to trace all of them yet. Some of these businesses are linked to key figures in Hereford, people we've overlooked so far."

Sara's gaze sharpened. "You think someone in Hereford has been protecting him?"

Lee nodded. "It makes sense. Kline didn't get to be this powerful on his own. He's been using local contacts to shield his operation, moving money through seemingly legitimate businesses. But we need proof."

"Okay, I think you're right. Let's start with the people we haven't looked at closely enough," Sara said. She reached into one of the boxes and removed one of the files. "Local politicians, business owners, anyone with a reason to want to protect Kline."

They began another deep dive into the hidden layers of Kline's network. As the hours passed, the web of corruption started to take shape. They uncovered dubious donations that had been made to city council members. Shady real estate deals involving prominent developers, a few of whom had been on Sara's radar for a while. Plus, several businesses that had benefited from Kline's influence. Throughout the secret documents, one name kept cropping up— Harold Blake, a wealthy developer with long-standing ties to Hereford's elite.

"Blake's been linked to Kline's businesses for years." Carla tapped the file she had in front of her. "They've worked on numerous projects together, and Blake's name also appears in some of the offshore accounts we've traced. Isn't that right, Lee?"

"Yep, there's no getting away from his involvement."

Sara narrowed her eyes. "Blake's a big name around here. If he's involved, that means Kline's influence could run even deeper than we thought. We'll need to handle this carefully."

"Blake's got connections to city council members, too," Carla added. "If he's been helping Kline cover up his money laundering operation, we'll need more than just suspicion to take him down."

Sara rubbed her temples, feeling the pressure of the investigation. Kline had built a fortress of corruption around himself, and Harold Blake was another key player in that system. If they intended to dismantle the operation, they had to take Blake down, too. Would the proof they'd uncovered so far be enough? Sara wasn't so sure, given his ties.

16

S ara had to ring Mark again to let him know that she would be working late for the second day running. He assured her that he was fine with her decision and that he would also be home late, as yet another emergency was due within the hour: a cat who had been run over.

At six-thirty, Sara prepared to confront Harold Blake. During the afternoon, the team had pulled out all the stops and gathered enough evidence to warrant questioning him. She knew this would be a pivotal moment. If Blake was involved, he could either provide the missing link they needed or further complicate an already dangerous situation.

Blake's estate in Mordiford could only be described as sprawling. An imposing mansion surrounded by high walls and security gates, which surprisingly opened when they approached. As they pulled up the long driveway, Sara's stomach churned with a mix of nerves and anticipation. People like Blake didn't usually cooperate willingly, so why welcome them without making a fuss?

"I'm not expecting this to be easy," Carla said, her voice low during the walk to the door. "Blake's got too much to lose."

"We've faced worse," Sara replied, her nerves spiking once more.

Sara inhaled a large breath and knocked on the huge oak door. A man wearing what appeared to be a butler's suit answered it.

He smiled warmly, except his eyes remained cold and unwelcoming. "Can I help you?"

Sara produced her ID. "DI Sara Ramsey and DS Carla Jameson. We'd like a quick chat with Mr Blake, if he's available?"

"He's expecting guests for dinner this evening. I'll have to check if he can spare five minutes or whether he would like to put a date in his diary to fit you in."

Sara pinned a smile in place. "The former would be preferable."

He invited them into the expansive hallway and asked them to wait. "I'll be right back. Please don't wander from this spot."

He walked away.

"Consider us told," Carla said behind her hand.

Sara quickly made a call to Barry. "We're in. The gates were opened for us. Check the perimeter for a way in. Come and get us if we're not out in twenty minutes. Heads up, he's expecting guests for dinner, so don't wander too far from the gates."

"Roger that, boss. Good luck."

She ended the call just before the butler returned.

"Mr Blake is willing to set aside ten minutes for you. Come this way, ladies."

He led them into Blake's grand office. The man himself was waiting for them: tall, broad-shouldered, with an air of arrogance that permeated the room. Harold Blake, in his tailored evening suit, exuded wealth and power. He assessed Sara and Carla, his eyes cold.

"The very best of evenings to you, ladies," Blake said smoothly. He motioned for them to take a seat. "To what do I owe the pleasure?"

Sara ignored his fake politeness, her intense gaze locking on his. "First of all, I wanted to thank you for agreeing to see us this evening, despite your imminent dinner arrangements." With a time constraint put on them, Sara got straight to the point. "We're investigating Victor Kline's criminal network, and your name has come up more than once."

Blake remained calm and collected. He raised an eyebrow and

beamed at them. "Kline? I know him, and I admit that I've done business with him in the past. Along with many other people in this county, I hasten to add, Inspector. That doesn't mean I'm involved in anything illegal."

"Perhaps you can tell me why some of your business transactions are linked to Kline's offshore accounts? FYI, that would be classed as an illegal transaction." She noted the shock register in his grey eyes. She continued to heap the pressure on him. "We've traced money flowing through several of your companies, and we have reason to believe you're guilty of protecting him."

Blake's smile faltered slightly, though he quickly recovered. "I assure you, any dealings I've had with Kline have been above board. My lawyers will confirm that."

Sara wasn't buying it. She ramped up the pressure. "This isn't just about business deals. You've been protecting Kline's money laundering operation, helping him move money through your projects. We have the records, and it's only a matter of time before we uncover the full extent of your involvement."

Blake's expression darkened, his charm slipping. "You're making a mistake, Inspector. I've been in this city longer than either of you, and I have connections that go much higher than you realise. I'm warning you, be very careful how you proceed."

His threat hung in the air, thick and suffocating. Sara's adrenaline pumped around her system, but she kept her expression neutral. "We'll see who has made the mistake."

Sara stood, and Carla followed her lead. As they turned to leave, Blake's voice stopped them.

"Inspector Ramsey, isn't it?" Blake shouted frostily. "I'd hate for your career to take a sudden turn for the worse. I have it on good authority that you're a force to be reckoned with. Trust me, you'd be wise not to make enemies out of me and my associates."

Sara's gaze held firm, though her stomach lurched. She'd dealt with threats before, but Blake's confidence unnerved her. He was dangerous, and he wasn't afraid to remind them of how far his reach went.

"We'll be in touch." Sara treated him to a cheeky confident wink and walked out of his office.

The butler was waiting in the hallway and escorted them to the front door. "Enjoy the rest of your evening, ladies."

"Don't worry, we will."

He opened the door. On the other side, a couple dressed in formal dinner attire were ascending the steps of the mansion. They seemed surprised to see them. Sara studied the visitors, but she didn't recognise them.

She brushed past them and flung over her shoulder, "I'd be careful who I mixed with if I were you."

"I beg your pardon," the gentleman retaliated tautly.

Sara smiled, descended the steps and made her way to the car with Carla close behind her. They reached the vehicle and looked back at the house.

"Did you recognise them?" Sara asked.

"Vaguely, although I'd have trouble putting a name to them."

"Let's hope the boys managed to get a photo of them as they drove in, so we can run it through the system."

"Too much to hope for," Carla said.

They slipped into the car, and Sara intentionally sped away to draw attention to themselves. "That'll give them something to talk about over dinner. Keep your phone handy. Snap any new arrivals on our way out."

Carla withdrew her phone the second a car came through the gates ahead of them.

Sara did what she could to hinder the car's approach, enabling Carla to take a photo of the driver and his passenger. Sara waved an apology to the angry driver and headed for the exit. They both laughed at her mischievous antics.

Sara spotted Barry's car up the road and flashed her lights. She drew up alongside him. "I don't suppose you caught the partygoers on camera, did you?"

Barry grinned. "As it happens, I did. How did it go?"

Sara waved her hand from side to side. "As expected. He's definitely involved. He appeared pig-sick when I mentioned Kline and the money laundering. We just need to build a case against him. We can start on that first thing. See you tomorrow." Sara raised her window.

Barry negotiated a three-point turn in the road and followed her back to the station.

Carla glanced over her shoulder at Blake's mansion. "We're getting close, Sara. But the closer we get, the more dangerous it is becoming."

"I know," Sara replied quietly. "But we can't back down now."

At the station, Sara wasn't ready to call it a day. Carla agreed to stay behind with her to review what they'd found on Blake so far. Together, they sifted through the evidence, and another piece of the puzzle fell into place. Carla found an email exchange between Blake and Kline that hinted at deeper involvement. The email contained some sort of coded language about transactions and 'mutual interests'.

Carla's eyes widened as she read the email. "This is it. This could turn out to be the final nail in both of their coffins."

Sara nodded, feeling a sense of satisfaction but also knowing that this investigation wasn't over yet. "We'll need to *invite* him in for questioning. Now that he knows Kline is in custody, Blake might panic."

Carla growled and pounded her fist into her palm. "We'll hit him with everything we've got," she said, her determination oozing out of every pore. "And when he breaks, we'll take down the rest of them."

Although Sara nodded, she couldn't shake the feeling of unease settling in her gut. Blake's warning echoed in her mind. They were getting closer to the truth, but who knew what danger lay ahead of them?

And if they weren't careful, the entire case could blow up in their faces.

17

Aware that the stakes were high, Sara tossed and turned all night long. In the end, keen not to disturb Mark, she spent the rest of the night in the spare bedroom with Misty. She found comfort in her cat's purring, which eventually helped her in her quest for sleep. The next morning, Sara prepared breakfast for herself and Mark, then showered and got dressed on autopilot. It wasn't until she saw the station on the horizon ahead of her that she realised she was in her car. *Jesus, how did that happen?*

She entered the main entrance, and a cheery Jeff greeted her.

"Good morning," she said. "You seem chirpy this morning. What's going on? Anything that I should know about?"

"You'll be pleased to know that Wheaton and Dobbs have both been arrested. Word has got around the station. As you can imagine, the shockwaves from the revelation that they are both bent coppers will remain with us for a long time. I've also made it clear that if anyone else intends to take backhanders or divulge information to criminals in the future, they will be dealt with accordingly." He shrugged. "The ball is in their court. If they want to say farewell to a decent early pension, then so be it."

Sara smiled. "You're one of the finest officers this station has ever seen, Jeff. Don't ever change."

He returned her smile. "I have no intention of ever changing, ma'am. I'm too old to start all that malarkey."

Sara winked and entered her code into the keypad. "I'll tell you something; dealing with all this shit this week has aged me ten years."

He nodded. "I can tell how stressful it has been for you. Don't forget, I'm always here if you need extra support. I know we've had a few issues with my staff this week. Hopefully, that's all behind us now."

"Don't worry, I'll shout if we need any extra help. See you later."

Carla entered the reception area before Sara had a chance to close the security door behind her. "You look rough, everything all right?"

"Thanks for the compliment. You don't look your usual cheerful self either."

Sara closed the door, and they continued their conversation during the trip to the incident room. "Lack of sleep tends to suck the life out of me."

"I hear you. I barely managed to get two hours myself last night."

"I suppose it shows we care."

"And some. What's on the agenda for today?"

"I'm going to try to interview Kline again. Although, I don't hold out much hope of him opening up to us. If he refuses to play ball, then we'll go ahead and charge him, get him on remand. See if a brief spell in prison will change his mind."

Carla laughed. "It does tend to do the trick with some criminals, not all of them, though."

"We'll see how that turns out. Then we need to concentrate on gathering more evidence to bring down Blake. When the team arrives, we'll get to work on that. I also need to get the photos that Barry snapped last night, as well as the ones you took."

"I'll get together with Barry and sort that out first thing, after we've thrown a mug of coffee down our necks. I think we'll both be relying on the caffeine to see us through the day, won't we?"

"I second that. You make the drinks, and I'll start on the post, not that I'm in the bloody mood for dealing with that onerous chore today."

As it was, there were fewer emails and letters for Sara to go through than normal. She glanced up at the sky and sent out a silent thank you to the universe for being on her side for a change. Ten minutes later, with her half-drunk coffee in hand, she rejoined the rest of her team.

"How did you get on?" she asked Carla.

"We believe the two couples were local property developers," Carla informed her. "We're still delving into their pasts. Should have some news for you soon on that front."

"That's excellent news. Well done, both of you." Sara crossed the room to the whiteboard and studied the photos and documents pinned to it. Harold Blake's smug face glared back at her, his connection to Victor Kline now undeniable. But the more they uncovered, the more dangerous she sensed the investigation was becoming. Blake's warning from the night before echoed in her mind, reminding her of the power he wielded.

She had faced powerful people before, but Blake was different. She regarded him as being in a league of his own. He wasn't just rich; he had deep connections within Hereford's political and business circles, and Sara had an inkling that those connections ran just as deep into the underworld. If they were going to bring him down, it would be down to her and the team to ensure the evidence they gathered was irrefutable.

Her thoughts were interrupted by Carla's arrival. She held out a folder for her to take. "You're going to want to see this," she said, her voice tight with urgency.

Sara looked up, her pulse quickening. "What have you found?" Sara opened the folder to reveal a series of bank records they hadn't known about.

"Blake's been busy. We've traced yet more offshore accounts, and they all lead back to him. He's been moving money through multiple shell companies, all laundered through legitimate businesses. There's no doubting it. Given this fresh information, he's definitely tied to Kline's entire operation—not just part of it, no matter what the tosser says. He's in deep."

Sara flipped through the records, her excitement rising. "This is it," she murmured. "We've got further proof, no, undeniable proof of a financial trail. Right, I'm calling it. We need to pick him up and bring him in for questioning. I doubt if he would honour a request to join us."

Carla nodded, but there was tension in her posture. "I agree, we have enough to make him squirm, but Blake's not the type to go down quietly. If we push him too hard, he's liable to retaliate. And who knows where that could lead?"

Sara perched on the desk beside her, her eyes narrowing. "There's no denying that Blake's dangerous, but we can't let that stop us. If we don't act now, he'll have time to cover his tracks."

They were walking into dangerous territory, and it felt as though Blake and possibly his numerous associates were waiting for them to make a wrong move.

The decision to bring in Blake wasn't made lightly. Sara and Carla prepared meticulously, going over every detail of the case. Every piece of evidence had to be thoroughly scrutinised to ensure there were no holes. Once they had Blake in custody, they couldn't afford for him to slip through their fingers.

The raid on Blake's estate was planned for that afternoon. The team gathered just after lunch, and Sara went over the strategy one final time. The tension was palpable, and Sara could feel the pressure of the situation mounting with each passing moment. This was a pivotal point in the investigation. If they succeeded, they would be able to dismantle Kline's entire network. If they failed, Blake would walk free, and Jessica would remain in danger, possibly for the rest of her life. The gravity of the situation was reflected in the team's expressions.

Sara stood at the front of the room, her tone steady and determined as she outlined the plan. "Blake's estate is heavily secured, but Judge Reynolds has pulled out all the stops for us again and granted us a warrant. We're going in with a full team. Jeff has agreed for six of his men to join us. We don't know how many people Blake has working for him. For all we know, he might have increased his security overnight since we visited his mansion, so stay alert. Once we have him, we'll bring him back to the station for questioning."

Sara's phone vibrated on the desk beside her. She glanced down, her heart skipping a beat when she saw it was from the officer in charge of Jessica's protection detail.

"DI Ramsey," she answered sharply.

"Sorry to trouble you, ma'am. We've had a situation. There was an attempt to breach the safe house."

Sara's blood ran cold. "Not again. What the fuck? What happened?"

"They didn't succeed. We've moved Jessica to a new location, but it was close."

"Send me the location. Is Jessica okay?"

"She's a bit shaken up, but otherwise fine. She's safe with us. I just thought you should be aware of the attempted abduction."

"How many were there?"

"Two men. We threatened them with our Tasers. They legged it over the fence and up a nearby alley. We could have given chase but were instructed to keep Jessica safe at all costs."

"Quite right. Thanks, keep your eyes and ears open. Don't let her out of your sight."

"Message received and understood, ma'am. You can trust us."

Sara hung up, wondering whether that was true or not. Blake's people were moving fast, proving to be relentless, targeting Jessica more aggressively.

"What's going on?" Carla asked, her brow furrowed with concern.

"There was an attempt on Jessica's safe house," Sara revealed.

"They didn't get through, but it's clear that Blake's upped the ante, determined to shut Jessica up, in one way or another."

Carla's jaw clenched. "Then we need to make our move, and quickly. Let's take him down before he has the chance to go after her again. I can't see him backing off, not while there's a breath left in his body."

The convoy of police vehicles drove swiftly through the outskirts of Hereford, heading to Blake's expansive estate in Mordiford. As they approached the gates, Sara's nerves buzzed with adrenaline. They had planned everything down to the last detail, but there was always the risk of something going wrong. Blake had untold resources available. It would be wrong of her not to believe he wouldn't anticipate what their next move would be.

The team gathered outside the gates, waiting for the go-ahead to breach the property. Sara stood beside Carla, studying the imposing mansion in the distance. Blake's wealth and influence were evident in every inch of the estate, but none of that mattered now. What mattered was getting to him before he had a chance to either flee or retaliate.

"All units ready?" Sara asked into her radio, receiving affirmatives from the teams scattered around the perimeter.

"Let's go."

The gates were forced open, and the Armed Response Team, who had volunteered to join them, quickly surrounded the estate. The officers fanned out, covering every possible exit, ensuring that no one could leave without being seen. Sara and Carla moved towards the main house, alert and scanning the grounds for any sign of Blake's security team.

The front door was locked, but the uniformed officers accompanying them used the enforcer to break it down. Inside, the mansion was eerily still. Sara gestured for everyone to remain quiet. She tilted her head to listen. Nothing. The Armed Response Team methodically searched the rooms, clearing each one during their advancement towards Blake's office.

As they neared the back of the house, Sara's stomach twisted into a large, suffocating knot. Something didn't feel right. The house was too quiet, too still, as if Blake had known they were coming.

They reached the heavy wooden door that led to Blake's office. Sara nodded to one of the officers, who kicked it open.

Surprisingly, they found Blake sitting at his desk, perfectly calm, his gaze casually rising from the papers in front of him. His lips curled into a sly smile.

"Inspector Ramsey. How nice to see you again, and so soon," he said smoothly. "Did you forget something last night?"

Sara's eyes narrowed. "You know why we're here, Blake. We've uncovered yet more evidence: offshore accounts, shell companies, the whole shebang. You've been laundering money through Kline's network for years, and now it's over."

Blake leaned back in his chair. Completely unfazed, he tapped his gold pen on his cheek. "You're making a huge mistake, Inspector. You won't find anything that ties me to Kline's illegal activities. I'm a businessman. My records are clean."

Sara shook her head and stepped forward, her gaze locked hard with his. "You're under arrest for your involvement in the money laundering operation. You'll have plenty of time to argue your innocence later."

Two officers stepped forward to cuff him. Blake didn't resist. He stood calmly, still smiling, intent on playing a game they hadn't figured out yet.

Blake was led out of the house. He peered over his shoulder and sneered, "You think you've won, don't you? But this is just the beginning. People like me don't crumble, Inspector. We wait. And when the time is right, we *strike!*"

Sara didn't flinch, but her insides reacted to the veiled threat. She knew better than to believe he was bluffing. Blake was powerful, and taking him down wouldn't be as simple as putting him behind bars.

Blake was loaded into the car. Carla exhaled a long-suffering breath. Lowering her voice, she said, "We've got him, but I don't like the way he's acting. It's as if he knows something we don't."

Sara nodded. The same thought had crossed her mind. "Blake's not done yet. We might have slapped the cuffs on him, but he's continuing to toy with us. This isn't over, not by a long shot. There's a truth behind his threats. He's not bluffing."

Once they reached the station, two uniformed officers removed Blake from the back of the car. Sara led the way into the reception area with Carla close behind her. The security door opened in front of them. Two officers escorted Kline out to the waiting police van they'd seen out front. Sara spun around to watch the interaction between the two men as they came face to face. She couldn't have timed their arrival better if she'd tried. She was shocked when Kline and Blake chose to ignore each other.

Kline was led out of the building. Blake stared at her, smiled and raised his eyebrows as if sending her a silent challenge.

The officers took him through to a holding cell. She'd let him sweat it out in there for a while, then contact his solicitor in half an hour or so, or whenever it suited her. She'd show him who was in control. But despite her cool exterior, Sara couldn't shake the feeling that they were still walking into a trap—that Blake had anticipated being brought in for questioning and was already planning his next move.

Upstairs, in the incident room, they went over what their next steps should entail. They had Blake in custody, but the fight was far from over. Their evidence had uncovered his vast network, and Sara knew they hadn't yet discovered all the players involved.

During their preparations for the interview, Sara's phone vibrated again. It was Ryan, the officer in charge of Jessica's new safe house.

"We've moved her to the second location," he reported. "But we've picked up chatter on the airwaves. Blake's people are still looking for her."

Sara's heart sank. Jessica wasn't safe. Not yet. When would this end?

"Keep her secure," Sara ordered, her voice steady despite the fear clawing at her. "We're getting closer, but I don't want to take any risks. We have the main man in custody. Once his men hear that, they're liable to react."

"Roger that, ma'am."

She hung up and faced Carla. "We need to move fast. Blake's people are still close, on the hunt for Jessica. If we don't take down the rest of his network soon, they'll find her."

Carla's eyes darkened with determination. "Then we need to break Blake during the interview. There's no way a man of his standing wouldn't have a plan in place for the possibility of his arrest."

Sara nodded, steeling herself for the next phase. They had Blake in custody, but the danger hadn't passed. If anything, it was growing stronger.

And now, it was up to her to outplay the cunning man. A man who, up until now, had spent his life winning.

18

Sara chose the interview room that required the most renovation just to piss off Blake and his solicitor. It was stark and cold, the type of room designed to strip away any sense of power or control. But as Sara stood behind the one-way glass, watching Harold Blake sit calmly at the metal table, it dawned on her that he wasn't like most suspects. He wasn't rattled in the slightest. In fact, he looked like a man who had been playing this game for a long time, and who wasn't used to losing.

Carla stood beside her, arms crossed, and sighed, venting her frustration. "He's too relaxed. It's like he knows that no matter what we throw at him, we're not going to get anywhere."

Sara nodded, focusing all her attention on Blake. "He's used to being in control. He thinks he's untouchable. But we're going to have fun changing that."

Carla turned to face her, a spark of determination lighting her eyes. "We need him to give us the rest of the names. If we don't, his people will keep going after Jessica. We both know he's still pulling the strings, even from in here."

"I know," Sara replied, her voice steady. "We're not going to let him get away with this. I'm determined to break him. Are you ready?"

They spent the next few seconds monitoring their breathing, inhaling and exhaling several times.

"I'm good to go."

Sara clenched her fists. "We've got this."

They left the room and entered the interview room next door, interrupting the conversation Blake was having with Mr Lawrence, his solicitor. Blake glanced up, and his gaze locked with Sara's, his lips curling into that all-too-familiar smirk.

"Inspector," he greeted her, his voice low and calm. "I was wondering how long it would take you to come to see us. Have you met Cyril Lawrence?"

"I haven't. Good of you to show up, Mr Lawrence." Sara dropped a file onto the table, intentionally causing the papers inside to spill out —bank records, photos, proof of his connection to the laundering operation. She tidied the contents and shoved them back into the file.

Carla recited the necessary verbiage for the recording.

Sara held Blake's gaze and stated confidently, "We have everything we need to take you down, Blake. You're not getting out of this."

He cocked an eyebrow, his smile never faltering. "Everything you need? I don't think so. You might have some documents, some numbers, but that doesn't mean I'll ever see the inside of a prison cell. People like me have..." he paused to wiggle his eyebrows, his smile broadening, "shall we say, ways of dealing with situations of this nature?"

Carla nudged Sara's knee, eager to get in on the act. She leaned forward, her voice cold and hard. "I wouldn't be so sure if I were you. We've tied you to Kline, and now that he's been shipped off on remand, we're going to unravel everything you've built. Your money, your reputation, it's all going to crumble."

Blake's eyes glinted with amusement. "You seem very confident, Sergeant, some would say too confident. But here's the thing—you have arrested Kline, but there's no sign of you catching anyone else. There are still people out there who owe me the odd favour or two. People who will make sure this little investigation of yours stumbles at the first hurdle."

Sara laughed and shook her head. "Words are cheap. We've got boxes of proof, highlighting the offshore accounts and the shell companies you've used to cover your illegal transactions. The paperwork dates back years. You made a mistake by going after Jessica Harding, fearing she was getting too close to blowing the whistle on your operation with Kline. You're not going to get out of this, Blake, and the sooner you realise that, the easier it will be."

Blake's smirk faded slightly, though he still seemed unfazed. "Jessica Harding," he mused. "Ah yes, the lawyer who thought she could play in the big league. It's a shame she didn't know when to stop. She could have been useful. She should have stayed quiet."

"Too bad for you, she didn't," Carla shot back. "She's still alive, and she's under our protection. She will testify against you and Kline, and when she does, every dirty deal you've ever made will be laid bare for all to see."

For a brief moment, Blake's eyes flickered with something undetectable—anger, perhaps, or fear—but it vanished just as quickly. He leaned back in his chair, his expression hardening, and crossed his arms. "Do you really think I'm afraid of that bitch's testimony? Jessica won't get the chance to say a word. I'll make sure of that."

Sara's heart skipped a beat, a tight knot forming in her stomach. "Yet another empty threat."

Blake's smile returned, more sinister now. "You think your little safe houses and protection teams are enough to stop the people I have working for me? Jessica's already as good as dead. And when she's gone, all your evidence dies with her."

Carla tensed beside her, her fists clenching. "You don't know what you're talking about."

"Oh, I think I do," Blake said, his voice dripping with arrogance. "You see, Detectives, I have a lot of resources at my disposal. And while you've been so focused on me, my people have been focused on one thing the last few days: finding that bitch. And believe me, my men are getting close."

Blake was taunting them, playing a psychological game that Sara had encountered numerous times over the years with spineless criminals in his position. It didn't stop his sinister words from unsettling her, though. *What if he's telling the truth? What if his people really are closing in on Jessica?*

She exchanged a glance with Carla, who nodded subtly. They needed to play this carefully.

Sara forced her shoulders back; her stance displayed a renewed confidence growing within. "You're bluffing. You don't know where she is. And even if you did, it's too late for you. You're going down, Blake. You'll never see the outside of a prison cell again."

Blake smiled and winked. "Bring it on, bitch. One of us is going to be proved wrong."

Sensing that they were going to continue going around in circles, Sara ended the interview, keen to put him back in a cell to see the impact that had on his mental status over time.

Lawrence tried to object. "This is absurd. I demand we continue with the interview. My client is a busy man. You have no right keeping him here."

Sara smiled and patted the file in front of her. "The proof tells us otherwise. Constable, can you escort Mr Blake back to his cell?"

Blake glared at her and shook his head. "You'd be wise not to mess with me, Inspector."

Sara stifled an exaggerated yawn. "I'm bored now. We'll interview you more in a few hours. We're conscious that the interview technique we adopt can be draining, therefore, we're giving you the opportunity to have a rest. Most *criminals* we interview would jump at the chance to have an early break."

The constable stepped forward and tapped Blake on the shoulder.

"Get your hands off me, you weasel."

Sara raised an eyebrow, amused that she'd succeeded in rattling him.

They followed Blake out of the room. His shoulders slumped, and Sara could tell his demeanour was rapidly changing.

Lawrence refused to shake Sara's hand when she took him back to the reception area.

Sara and Carla returned to the incident room, both deep in thought. Blake was dangerous, more dangerous than Sara had initially thought. He wasn't just a businessman protecting his empire. He'd already proven that he was willing to go to any lengths to ensure Jessica was silenced.

"Do you think he's bluffing?" Carla asked.

"I don't know," Sara admitted. "But I'm not prepared to take the risk. We need to make sure Jessica is safe, transfer her to another location, if we have to."

Carla nodded. "I'll call the team. We'll double her protection and switch locations. If Blake's people are getting close, we need to stay one step ahead of them."

Sara's phone rang in her pocket, pulling her attention away from the conversation. She peered at the screen and froze. It was a message from Jeff on the reception desk.

We've lost contact.

Sara's heart skipped several beats. She quickly dialled the number of the officer protecting Jessica, her hands shaking as the phone rang.

No answer.

"What's wrong?" Carla asked.

"It was Jeff. They've lost contact with Jessica's team," Sara said, panic rising within.

Carla's face paled. "How long ago?"

Sara didn't respond. She rushed towards the door, her mind spinning with fear. If Blake had been telling the truth, if his people were already moving in, Jessica's life was in immediate danger.

Carla shouted, "Wait for me."

They tore down the stairs. The protection team's location was only a few miles away, but the distance felt like an eternity as they sped through the streets, sirens blaring.

"Slow down. She'll be okay," Carla muttered, as if trying to convince herself. "There's probably a reasonable explanation for their radio silence."

Sara didn't respond. She couldn't. Her mind was too focused on what they would find when they arrived. She wanted to bash the side of her head to stop Blake's words from reverberating—his smug confidence that Jessica was already as good as dead.

They drew up outside the safe house, the scene disconcertingly quiet. The front door was slightly ajar.

"Shit, I don't like the look of this. Be careful," she warned Carla, her hand resting on her Taser. They left the car and approached the house.

Inside, the living room was in disarray, with furniture overturned and papers scattered everywhere. There had clearly been a struggle. Sara's breath caught in her throat. They rushed through the house, calling out for the officers assigned to protect Jessica.

But there was no response.

When they reached the back room, Sara's blood ran cold.

The officers were unconscious, sprawled on the floor, blood staining their clothes. Jessica was nowhere to be found.

"No, no, no..." Carla muttered. She knelt beside one of the officers to check his pulse. Then she shuffled over to the second man to check his. "Phew! They're both alive, but barely."

Sara stood there, glued to the spot, dread sweeping through her. Jessica was gone.

Blake's people had abducted her... again, just like he'd said they would.

"Get the medics over here," Sara shouted into her radio, her voice trembling. "And we need to find Jessica. Now."

Carla stood, her face void of colour and grim. "Blake was right. How? How have they got to her? Shit, shit, shit! I can't believe they've taken her again."

Sara's chest tightened with fear and fury. Jessica was in the hands of these evil bastards, and she had no idea where they had taken her.

"We'll find her," Carla said. She threw an arm around Sara's shoulder, and they rested their foreheads against each other's in defeat. "We have to."

But Sara couldn't shake the sinking feeling that this time would be different.

And now, it was a race against the clock to save Jessica before someone pulled the trigger for real this time. Could this day get any worse? She detested the thought of Blake sitting in his cell and laughing at them.

19

The clock was ticking, and the atmosphere in the station was full of foreboding. Jessica was missing, again, taken by Blake's evil men. Sara struggled to rid herself of the horrific images of what Jessica's captors could be doing to her right now. If she was still alive. Every second that passed felt like sand slipping through her fingers, and she couldn't stop replaying the scene at the safe house: the unconscious officers, the signs of a struggle, and the eerie quiet that had followed.

Carla was scanning the map of Hereford on the desk, marking possible locations where Blake's people could have taken Jessica. Although they had already raided Blake's estate, the problem was that his network still had deep roots running throughout Hereford and beyond. The longer Jessica was missing, the more dangerous the situation became.

"We've got patrols searching the usual places," Carla muttered, her voice tight as she worked. "But Blake's people are smart. They've been one step ahead of us this whole time."

Sara nodded, barely hearing her. Her mind was on Jessica, considering how terrified she must be, after all she had been through. "We've let her down. I'm never going to be able to forgive myself. I promised to protect her, to keep her safe, and now Jessica is in the hands of the very people we've been trying to stop. How could that happen?" She let out an exasperated growl. "We're missing something." She paced in front of the whiteboard. "Blake wouldn't have taken her somewhere obvious. He's too clever. This time, he'd want to make sure we couldn't find her... until it's too late."

Carla glanced at her. "Blake's the type of bastard to play mind games with us. We've got to stay ahead of him. Think like he does. Where would he hide her? Somewhere we wouldn't think to look."

Sara's phone rang on the desk beside her, pulling her out of her thoughts. She snatched it up, her heart pounding as she saw the caller ID. It was one of the analysts she'd called in to specifically assess Kline's financial records. "Inspector Ramsey," she answered, detesting the sound of desperation in her tone.

"It's Alan. I heard the news. It's rife around the station. I took it upon myself to look over Kline's property portfolio, just in case. I know the two of them are as thick as thieves. Anyway, there's one we hadn't flagged before." He paused to take a breath. "It's an old warehouse, registered to a shell company under a different name. I would class it as an ideal hiding place."

"I'm listening. Where is it, Alan?"

"It's remote. On the outskirts of town. And it's the only property we haven't raided yet."

Sara's pulse quickened. "Sounds plausible. Will you send us the coordinates? It's worth us taking a punt. We'll head over there now. Thanks, Alan."

"I'll keep digging. Good luck. Let me know if you find her."

"I will, and thanks again." Sara hit the END CALL button and punched the air. But reprimanded herself. It wasn't a definite location, only a possibility at this stage.

Carla glanced up, her brow furrowed. "Have you got something?"

"Alan heard the news and did some extra digging into Kline's properties, and he thinks he's come up trumps with a warehouse," Sara said. She made her way into her office to collect her jacket. When she returned, she added, "It's remote, registered under a shell company. We haven't been there yet, but if Blake's men took Jessica, they're probably aware of that. It might be where they're keeping her."

The whole station was on high alert.

Carla got to her feet and notified Jeff. "We've got to go there prepared. If they've got her, we need to be ready for anything."

By the time they had collected their Tasers from the armoury, the reception area was flooded with uniformed officers.

Jeff was in the process of laying the law down to them. "What Inspector Ramsey and Sergeant Jameson say goes. If I hear of anyone disrespecting them or trying to do their own thing at the location, you'll have me to deal with." He placed his flattened hand above his head. "And I've had it up to here with my men letting me down."

Sara knew he was referring to Wheaton and Dobbs, the two moles they'd uncovered. She scanned the sea of faces ahead of her and wondered how many other officers in the room could be bought. She shook her head. She had enough rumbling around in her mind at the moment, without dealing with that added complication.

The convoy of police vehicles, headed up by Sara, tore through the streets of Hereford, their lights cutting through the darkness as they raced towards the warehouse. Sara's adrenaline pumped through her veins, a mixture of fear and determination propelling her forward. She had made a conscious effort to block out the images of what Blake's men might do to Jessica. Instead, she directed her focus towards saving her, and getting there before it was too late.

Carla was beside her, her fists clenched in her lap. "We've got to hit them hard from the get-go," she said. "I fear what will happen to Jessica if we hold off. We can't allow them time to react." She slammed her fists on her thighs.

Sara nodded. Her breathing had altered. It was coming in short, sharp bursts. "You're right. We can't lose her, Carla. Not again. This time, we grab her, and I'm not going to let her out of our sight until we round up all of Blake's men."

"Jesus, that could take a while, Sara."

"I know, but what other options do we have? You saw what happened to the two officers protecting her: both are in hospital beds with head injuries."

Carla sighed and unclenched her fists. "We're two minutes away."

The surrounding landscape became more desolate the closer they got to the warehouse. Dozens of abandoned buildings and empty lots stretched for miles. It was the perfect place for someone to hide, to disappear with no one noticing.

"What a waste? Look at it. The council should be developing this area, or at least allow developers to buy it."

"Yep, it would definitely make a dent in the shortage of houses in the area."

Sara drew the car to a halt around fifty feet from the warehouse. The team of officers joined them and, in force, with their Tasers drawn, Sara gestured for them to make their move. Before they could take a step, another vehicle joined them. Sara smiled, realising who the vehicle belonged to.

A man stepped out and approached the group. "We thought you might need a helping hand, Inspector."

Sara placed a hand over her chest, surprised and delighted to see the ART inspector. "Any help you and your men can offer is fine by me."

"You take the lead. Let us know when you want us to make our move."

"Thanks. Let's go. We'll split up when we get closer, surround the building before we hit them."

The team all murmured their understanding.

"My partner and I will go in fast," Sara whispered, her voice steady. "No hesitation."

Carla gave her a sharp nod. "Let's do this."

Two officers broke down the door, and the team charged through the warehouse. Inside, the space was dimly lit, the air heavy with the scent of oil and dust. Sara's eyes adjusted quickly. She scanned the shadows, her senses on high alert. Every second mattered.

The closer they got, the more Sara picked up on the faint sound of voices. She signalled for the team to stop, but her heart rate escalated as she strained to listen.

"We need to get her shifted soon," a man's gruff voice said. "I wouldn't put it past that bitch of an inspector to show up here mob-handed. I've dealt with her in the past. She's not one we should be taking lightly. I don't care what Blake or Kline say. Some coppers can't be bought. She's a stickler for keeping within the rules."

Sara grinned at the man's accurate assessment of her. He was right: she couldn't be bought.

She held a finger to her lips and motioned for the team to get closer, inching towards the source of the voices. Tension filled every step, bringing them closer to the confrontation they knew was coming.

Then Sara saw them: two men standing by a small makeshift holding area in the corner of the warehouse. And there, tied to a chair, was Jessica.

Sara's heart leapt into her throat. She was alive.

Jessica's head was slumped forward, her hair covering her face, but the rise and fall of her chest came as a huge relief. Sara's grip on her Taser tightened and she exchanged a glance with Carla.

"We should take them now," Carla whispered.

Sara shook her head. "No, it's too dangerous. They're too close to her. We were lucky last time with Kline. I can tell these bastards mean business. One false move from us and they might kill her."

"What are you saying?"

Sara gestured for Dave Salter, the inspector of the Armed Response Team, to join them. He was light-footed, stealth-like in his movement. "What do you need?"

Sara urged him to look through the gap. "I think you should take over."

He nodded. "I agree. Let us deal with the bastards." He organised his team and counted down with his raised fingers, then burst into the room.

"Police! Drop your weapons!" Dave shouted.

Chaos broke out. Sara was terrified that the men would put a bullet in Jessica before they were captured.

One of the men reached for his gun. A single shot rang out, and the man crumpled to the floor, his weapon skittering away. The second man froze, his hands shooting above his head as he stared at the armed team surrounding him.

Dave nodded, giving Sara the all-clear. She rushed to Jessica's side, her hands trembling as she knelt beside her. "Jessica, can you hear me?"

Jessica groaned softly. Her eyes took a few seconds before they fluttered open. She looked up at Sara, her face pale and bruised, relief flooding her eyes. "Sara..."

Sara's throat tightened. She quickly untied her and drew Jessica into a protective embrace. "You're safe now. We've got you."

Jessica clung to her, her voice trembling. "I thought... I thought they were going to kill me. They said it was only a matter of time."

"Not on my watch," Sara whispered fiercely.

To their right, Carla stood over the captured man, her Taser trained on him. "You're going to tell us what you know or spend your life in prison."

The man glared at her, his eyes narrowing, but he said nothing.

Carla shrugged. "Suits me. You've had your chance. We'll deal with you back at the station."

When they arrived at the station, the duty doctor was called, and she came almost immediately. Sara and Carla stood outside the room, their hearts still racing from the intensity of the rescue. But even with Jessica safe, they knew this wasn't over.

"We got her back," Carla said quietly. "But Blake's still got someone out there, ensuring his orders are carried out."

Sara nodded, her face grim. "And I'm guessing they won't stop until either they kill her or we take them all down. We've got two of the big players in custody. There has got to be another big name pulling the strings."

"You're right, but who?"

"Maybe we can get the information out of the man we've just brought in." Sara puffed out her cheeks. It had been another long day, and she couldn't see it ending soon.

"What are we going to do about Jessica?"

"I'll have a word with Jeff and see if he has got a spare female officer who can sit with her for a while. That'll leave us to conduct the interview. I'll worry about what to do with her afterwards."

Sara left Carla guarding the room and went back to the reception area. She ran the idea past Jeff.

"Leave it with me. I think Fiona is due back from her break soon."

"Cheers, Jeff. You're a good 'un."

Sara returned to share the good news with Carla. "How are you holding up?"

"I'm tired, but the adrenaline is keeping me going. Don't worry about me. What about you?"

"The same. Shit, I should have rung Mark a while ago." She stepped away to make the call in private.

"Where the hell are you, Sara? I've been going out of my mind. You usually call me if you're going to be late."

"I know. It's been a full-on day, and it's not over yet. Please forgive me, Mark. You know I usually keep you informed."

"Okay, okay. Are you all right?"

"Yes, pumped and ready to go again. I'll explain all when I see you. I can't tell you when that will be, though, sorry."

"It's okay. I know you're dealing with an important case."

She lowered her voice and said, "I love you."

"Ditto. Let me know what's going on later, if you can."

"I will. I promise."

She ended the call, and her phone immediately jangled. A message from the analyst had arrived.

· · ·

THE NET IS CLOSING **in on them. We've uncovered more accounts. It has also highlighted that Blake's network is bigger than we thought.**

SARA'S STOMACH CHURNED. Blake's influence reached further than they had realised, and now it was clear that taking him down wouldn't be as simple as locking him up.

She wandered over to stand alongside her partner and rested her back against the wall.

"Blake's playing a bigger game than we thought," Sara muttered. "We need to find the rest of his network before they regroup."

Carla nodded, her eyes dark with determination. "Let's break this guy. We'll make him talk. Maybe dangle a deal in front of him. What do you think?"

"It's got to be worth a try."

A female officer walked towards them. "Hello, ma'am. I'm Fiona. The desk sergeant told me to come and find you."

"Thanks. I want you to guard Jessica Harding. No one speaks to her without me knowing first. She's been abducted several times over the last few days. I'm determined it won't happen again."

"The sergeant has made me aware of the situation. You can trust me, ma'am."

"That's good to hear. The doctor is with her at the moment..."

With that, the door opened, and the female doctor joined them.

"How is she, Doctor?" Sara took a step forward to ask.

"She's in shock and in dire need of rest. She's asking to go home, to be with her husband."

Sara shook her head. "Sorry, that's not going to happen. We can't take the risk. There are people out there who are trying to take her life. They're probably watching her home as we speak."

The doctor shrugged. "You know what's best. That woman needs complete and utter rest. She's been through an horrendous ordeal."

"I know. Leave it with us. We'll get something sorted."

The doctor smiled and went back to the reception area.

"This is a bit out of the box," Carla said, "but why don't we lock her up in a cell? We can give her a few extra home comforts to compensate for it, but at least we know she'll be safe."

Sara weighed up the idea for a moment and then nodded. "If she's agreeable to it. Nip back and have a word with Jeff, will you, Fiona?"

The young officer hurried up the hallway. Sara and Carla entered the room.

Jessica glanced up, wide-eyed, clearly still in shock. "I want to go home," she whispered.

"I'm sorry, Jessica, we can't let you go home, not yet. We need to keep you safe."

Jessica stared at Sara and said, "How has that worked out so far?"

Sara sighed and shrugged. "I admit, up until now we've let you down. Which is why we've come up with a plan, although I don't think you're going to like it."

"Go on."

"The doctor told us that you need complete rest. Umm... my suggestion would be that you stay in a cell overnight."

"What? Is this some kind of joke?"

"No, I'm deadly serious. We can't force you, obviously, but if you don't... there's no telling whether Blake might send more of his goons to abduct you again."

"Not a great option to be given. However, I understand what you're saying. Okay, for one night, only because I'm too exhausted to argue."

"We'll throw in some extra home comforts, I promise."

"Does that include a takeaway from my favourite fine dining restaurant?"

"Umm..."

"I was teasing. Fish and chips from the local chippy will suffice."

"Give me ten minutes to get things sorted for you." What Sara neglected to tell her was that Blake would be residing in a nearby cell.

There were times in life when it was necessary to hide the truth. This was one of those occasions.

WITH JESSICA safely tucked away in her cell, eating her well-deserved fish and chips, Sara turned her attention to interviewing Todd Norris, one of the goons who had held Jessica hostage. The duty solicitor, Mr Yeoman, had arrived and was briefing Norris.

Sara and Carla entered the room. Carla started the recording. She announced who was present, then sat back, allowing Sara to take over. Aware they were up against it, time wise, Sara decided to hit Norris hard and fast. At first, he gave the usual criminal-up-shit-creek response, 'no comment'.

"Fine, keep going down that route, you're not doing yourself any favours."

He folded his arms and grinned at her. "No comment."

She'd had enough. Her patience wearing thin, she slammed her fists on the table and glared at him. "You've got a final chance," Sara said coldly. "Tell us where the rest of Blake's people are. We know you're part of the operation. If you cooperate, we can work something out. But if you don't..."

Norris' jaw clenched, but his mouth remained shut.

Sara nudged Carla under the table, giving her the go-ahead to try to crack him.

Carla leaned in, her voice low and menacing. "You've seen what we can do. We'll find the others involved, with or without your help. But if you help us, the inspector has already hinted that there's a deal to be had."

Norris shrugged nonchalantly, but Sara recognised a glint of consideration in his eyes. He hesitated for a long moment, then finally relented.

"There's a location... an old estate just outside the city. That's where Blake's real operation is run from. The money, the accounts... everything's managed from there."

Sara exchanged a quick glance with Carla. This could be the break they needed.

"Give us the address," Sara demanded. She slid her notebook across the table.

Norris scribbled down the location, his hands shaking, probably scared of the consequences. He gulped and returned the notebook to Sara. "You didn't hear it from me."

"Don't worry, your secret is safe with us. Glad you saw sense, eventually." She gestured for the officer at the back of the room to take Norris to his cell.

"Don't forget the deal you put on the table," Norris shouted over his shoulder. "Make sure she sticks to her word," he told the solicitor.

"Unlike you and your associates, I never go back on my word," Sara called after him.

She shot out of her chair and rushed upstairs with Carla close on her tail.

After obtaining her second wind, Sara moved quickly to assemble the team. Now that they finally had the location of Blake's main operation, Sara was eager to seize the opportunity to take down the entire network once and for all. "I know it's late and we're keen to get home, but I feel if we delay the raid until tomorrow, it might work against us."

Carla stretched her arms above her head and yawned. "Let's finish what we started."

With the team behind them, they headed out to the address that they had been reliably informed housed Blake's operation. Sara knew the importance behind this raid. Although the fight was far from over, they had a real chance to end the operation and ensure Jessica's safety.

And this time, Sara was determined they wouldn't leave any loose ends.

20

The team arrived at the location on the outskirts of Hereford. This time, Sara had put in the request for the Armed Response Team to assist them. She was exhausted, dead on her feet, and she said as much to Inspector Salter when she handed the reins over to him.

"I can tell. Leave it to me. Hopefully, we'll be in and out within the next half an hour."

"Did you know about this place?"

"Nope. I didn't even know it existed. You can see why the criminals chose the location."

"I certainly can. Good luck."

He smiled, nodded and gathered his team. After running through a proposed plan, he signalled for his men to spread out. They surrounded the building, a smaller warehouse than the others they'd raided over the past few days.

Sara and Carla linked arms and watched on in silence. Shots rang out. Shouts from the armed officers echoed throughout the building until silence descended. Moments later, a lone figure appeared by the main door, shining a torch in their direction, urging them to join him.

Sara and her team ran towards the building, their Tasers secured in their pockets. "What have you got?"

"Why don't you come and see for yourself?"

The armed team stood in a circle, and three men lay facedown on the floor. Over to the right, what appeared to be an incinerator bin was alight.

"Shit, how much have they destroyed?"

Dave shrugged. "They're refusing to tell us."

Frustration coursed through her veins. With determination, Sara pushed through the crowd, snatched a tuft of hair from one of the suspects and forcefully pulled his head backwards. "How much have you burnt?"

He grinned, showing off nicotine-stained teeth. "Wouldn't you like to know?"

She released his head and, without thinking, kicked him in the side.

"Hey, you can't do that. I'll do you for assault."

"Shut the fuck up," Dave warned him. "Or I'll stick my boot in as well, only my shoes have reinforced toes. Now answer the question. How much have you got rid of?"

"A boxful, that's all. We only arrived half an hour ago."

In the meantime, Carla and the rest of the team had crossed the room to assess the contents of the files.

Sara joined them. "What have you got, anything?"

Carla winked and clicked her tongue. "Looks like the missing pieces of the puzzle to me."

Sara rested her head on Carla's shoulder and closed her eyes. "Thank fuck for that. Barry, can you organise a van to come and pick this lot up?"

"On it, boss." He exited the building to make the call.

"We'll wrap things up and get out of here, unless you still need us?" Dave said.

"No, we're fine. The men have been handcuffed, haven't they?"

"All done. We can get them outside for you, no problem."

Sara smiled. "If you wouldn't mind, that'd be great."

Barry returned and told her that a van was on the way.

Half an hour later, they left the location and returned to the station. Sara banged up the three men in the cells for the night, intending to interview them first thing with the rest of her team.

The van was unloaded, and yet more boxes were taken upstairs.

"Barry, shove them in my office for now. I can lock the door overnight, just in case."

"Will do, boss."

When the process had been carried out, Sara glanced around her team and applauded them. "Well done on a job expertly carried out. Now go home and get some rest."

Her colleagues smiled, appreciating her congratulations, and drifted off. Only Carla remained behind. She approached Sara.

"I know we're both desperate to get out of here, but I can't resist having a quick shufty in the boxes."

Sara sniggered. "You read my mind."

They entered her office. She opened one of the boxes and sifted through the files. One of them caught her eye. "Hmm... TOP SECRET, I wonder what we're going to find in here."

Carla crossed her fingers and held them up. "Hopefully, it'll be a list of names. The other members involved in the operation."

Sara opened the file. Carla was right. It consisted of two full pages listing important businessmen and women in the area.

"What the fuck? Yes, we've got them bang to rights now." Legs shaking, Sara was tempted to take a seat. She tottered slightly, and Carla had to reach out to support her.

"You're knackered. We both are. Why don't we leave it for tonight?"

"If I do that, I probably won't be able to sleep. I'll take the file home and study it."

Carla tutted and raised an eyebrow. "Mark is going to love that."

Sara grinned and pulled back her shoulders. "Leave him to me. He'll be putty in my hands. Come on, let's get out of here."

.   .   .

While she drove home, she kept looking sideways at the folder on the passenger seat beside her.

Mark was pleased to see her. He frowned when he spotted the file she was carrying. "I can't believe you would bring work home with you. Don't you think you've worked long enough today as it is, Sara?"

"Please don't start on me." She explained the situation, about what they'd discovered in the raid and how late it had been when they had found the file. "Curiosity has got the better of me. I'll take a cursory glance through it, that's all, I promise. How was your day?"

"Hectic," he said in a huff and walked away from her.

"Mark, please don't be like this."

"Like what? You promised me this wouldn't happen. We both work exceptionally hard. We should be able to come home at night and leave our working lives behind us. You don't seem capable of doing that lately. Do you want your dinner? Hopefully, it's not ruined."

"I'd love it and I'm sorry. I know we made a pact. You know how important this case is, though." She waved the file at him. "This could be the icing on the cake for us. The damning proof that could put away dozens of corrupt people in this city."

He removed the piping-hot shepherd's pie from the oven with a cloth and placed it on the wicker placemat at the table. Ignoring her statement, he left the room and muttered, "Enjoy," as he walked through the doorway.

Sara was caught between a rock and a hard place. Did she leave him to cool down and eat her meal, the smell of which was making her stomach rumble and reminding her that she hadn't stopped for lunch during the day? Or did she go after him? A couple of torturous moments passed before she decided to eat her meal, allowing Mark to chill while she ate.

She collected some cutlery from the drawer and settled down. The dinner was still too hot for her to attempt to eat. Instead, she flipped open the file and cast her eyes down the list of names. It didn't take her long to become engrossed in her work.

Mark stuck his head into the room a little while later and caught her. "Jesus, Sara, you haven't even touched your dinner. Fuck, I give up. I'm going for a pint. I need some space."

"Mark, I'm sorry. Come back, don't be like this, please."

The door rattled in its frame. She shook her head, mortified by his behaviour. This was totally out of character for him. She tried to eat her meal, but the food couldn't get past the lump in her throat. Sara picked up the file again and turned the page. One name on the sheet of paper drew her attention like a flashing beacon.

"What the fuck!"

She slammed the file shut, stunned by what she'd read. She attempted to eat a mouthful of her food but ended up spitting it out again, then threw it in the bin. She searched for some old letters she could throw away to hide the evidence from Mark, not wanting to make him angrier than he already was.

After washing up, she poured herself a glass of wine, let Misty out and fed her, then took her wine and the file up to bed with her.

Mark came home an hour later. He stomped his way up the stairs and appeared in the doorway. "I'm sorry."

"What for? I'm the one who should be apologising, not you. We had an agreement, and I've broken it more than once this week. That is unforgivable of me." She had heard him coming and shoved the file under the bed.

He came towards her, his arms open wide, wanting a cuddle. "I don't know what's wrong with me lately."

"I do. You've had major surgery, and you're also grieving the loss of your dear mother. That's bound to have an effect on you, sweetheart."

"That was a few months ago. I should be back to normal by now. I hear myself having a go at you, and I try to stop it but fail every time."

"If something is bothering you, it's better to get it off your chest. We both know that."

He rested his head on her shoulder and sobbed. "I didn't get to see her as often as I would have liked, but it's hit me so hard, Sara. I miss her so much. The fact that I can no longer call her out of the blue is difficult. I find myself daydreaming at work, standing in the middle of my surgery, not knowing what day of the week it is or what I'm doing there. Grief sucks."

"I know it does. I felt the same when my mum passed. It's going to take time to heal. I'm right here. I'll always be here beside you. Why don't you consider taking a couple of days off to visit your father? That might help."

"Maybe. I'll have a think about it. I suppose I'm worried about him as well. Every time I call him, he tells me he's coping, but I'm sensing he isn't, not at all. They were together nearly forty years."

"It's got to be tough on both of you. Perhaps we can visit him over the weekend. Damn, no, we can't, Dad has invited us for dinner. I could postpone, put it off until next weekend. I'm sure he wouldn't mind in the circumstances."

"No, don't do that. We'll visit Dad next week instead. Thanks for understanding, Sara. I love you."

"Not as much as I love you." She clung to him until he pulled away and kissed the tip of her nose. Then he went into the bathroom and had a shower.

They cuddled and kissed until Mark fell asleep. Sara's mind continued to buzz, going over the ramifications of the facts she'd discovered and would need to act upon in the morning.

21

Mark was like a different person the following morning, more like his old self. Sara was pleased that he had opened up to her the night before. He kissed her goodbye and apologised as they got in their respective vehicles to leave for work. She promised to call him at lunchtime, like she usually did.

The closer she got to the station, the more her trepidation intensified. She glanced sideways at the file and shook her head. "Shit, shit, shit!"

Carla was getting out of her car when she drew into her parking space. Her partner wandered over to greet her. "Good morning. I hope you slept well last night."

"Sort of. You're going to have to hold the morning meeting for me. I need to see the chief first thing. There's something urgent I have to bring to her attention."

Carla narrowed her eyes. "Something you discovered in the file last night?"

Sara held the folder tightly to her chest and nodded. "You could say that. Can you also call the duty solicitor? We'll let Barry and Craig interview the three men we arrested last night."

"Oh, right. Okay, that's fine by me, if you think we're going to be needed elsewhere. God, I hate all this secrecy. Can't you just tell me what's going on?"

Sara heaved out a sigh. "Trust me, Carla, let me see the chief first and then I'll reveal all."

"Whatever," Carla said. She turned her back on Sara and stomped off.

Sara could cope with her partner going off in a huff; it allowed her the headspace to deal with what lay ahead of her. She entered the station and high-fived the desk sergeant. "We did it, Jeff. I appreciate all the help you've given me this week."

"Always here for you, ma'am. Always eager to lend a hand to my favourite inspector."

She smiled. "Excuse me, I have a date with destiny that I have to deal with first thing."

He cringed. "Ouch, sounds ominous."

She ran her fingers over her lips as if to zip them shut. He raised his thumb in acceptance. Sara punched in her code and climbed the stairs. With each step she took, her legs felt as if heavy weights were attached to them. Instead of turning left at the top of the stairs, she went right towards the chief's office.

Mary was busy setting up the coffee machine when she arrived. "Oh, hello, Inspector. What can I do for you?"

"I need to see the chief urgently. Is she available?"

"She's just arrived. Let me see if she can see you now."

"Thanks, Mary."

The secretary knocked on the chief's door and slipped inside the room. She reappeared a few seconds later and held the door open for Sara to enter. Sara's feet felt glued to the spot. It took a massive effort to get her legs working again. When she entered the room, she found the chief going through her post.

"Hello, Sara. This is a surprise. What can I do for you?"

Sara smiled and approached her boss's desk. She threw the file on top of the post.

DCI Price stared at the file and then glanced up at Sara. "What's this?"

"A list of names of individuals involved in Kline and Blake's huge operation. Open it, take a gander at the second page. I've highlighted the name that has drawn my attention the most."

Carol Price frowned and followed her instructions.

Carol slammed the file shut and sat back in her chair. "I can explain."

"What the fuck? You're the mole. How could you?"

"It's not what it looks like, Sara. Please, you have to believe me. Take a seat. Let's talk about this."

Sara dropped into the seat beside her, not because her boss had told her to, but because her legs could no longer hold her weight. She folded her arms and glared at her boss, her mentor, the woman she'd looked up to all these years. "I repeat, how could you?"

Tears welled up in her boss's eyes.

Sara wagged her finger. "You don't get to show emotion, expecting me to feel sorry for you. I demand to know why," she shouted through gritted teeth. Her immediate superior needed to know how much trouble she was in and that Sara wasn't about to go easy on her. She could see the cogs turning in the chief's mind. "Now, reveal the truth without the need to come up with a despicable lie. You owe me that much. Jesus, I feel sick to my stomach right now knowing the secrets I've divulged to you over the years, both personally and professionally, only to realise that you've probably set out to use them against me."

Price shook her head. She sat forward and interlocked her fingers on the desk. "I haven't, I swear. Anything you've confided in me has remained between us."

"Bollocks! Do you really expect me to believe that bullshit when all along Blake and Kline have had you on speed dial? I've never detested someone as much as I detest you right now. Have the courage to tell me the truth. Tell me why you've continually put Jessica Harding's life in danger this week."

Price broke down and sobbed. Sara felt nothing as she watched the chief's pitying act.

"They had... something over me..."

"What could they possibly have had over a DCI, who, may I remind you, swore an oath to the crown of this country?"

The door opened, and Mary entered the room.

"Get out," Price shouted.

The tray Mary had been holding clattered to the floor, and she fled the room.

"Don't take it out on her. She's done nothing wrong," Sara warned.

"I'm sorry. This can all be explained if you give me the opportunity, Sara."

"Go on, I'm listening. Keen to hear the truth. Don't bother lying. I'm experienced enough to know when someone is pulling the wool over my eyes during an interview." And yet, that's exactly what Price had successfully done to her for years.

"Cards on the table. I don't see the point in denying it any longer. In fact, I'm relieved the truth has come out. Blake has been blackmailing me for years."

"Bullshit!"

The chief's eyes widened. "It's the truth," she snapped back.

"How is that possible?"

"Years ago, he owned a casino. I went along with my friends one night, liked it and went back on my own. I lost a lot of money. He was watching me on the cameras, aware of who I was. He agreed to wipe off the debt. I thought that would be the end of it. However, once the debt was cleared, he dropped by my house for a visit. He laid it on the line what was expected of me and what would happen to me if I didn't comply with his wishes."

Sara shook her head. "You fell for it. Despite having the law on your side, you allowed him to blackmail you. You are aware that's a criminal offence right there, aren't you?"

"Don't treat me like an idiot, Sara. Of course I'm aware."

"How much did you owe him?"

The chief's eyes closed. "A quarter of a million. It was either that or hand over the keys to my house. What would you have done in my situation?"

Sara wagged her finger again. "I wouldn't have been seen dead in a casino in the first place. No good ever comes of people who choose to spend time there, as you've just admitted. Surely you could have reached out to someone about this. Spoken to the superintendent."

Price ran a hand through her hair. "Can you imagine the embarrassment?"

Sara had heard enough. She slammed her fist on the desk. "You disgust me. You're a selfish bitch. So, what you're telling me is that you'd rather put other people's lives in jeopardy than deal with the embarrassment of being in debt."

"I'm sorry." Price broke down, covering her face with her hands when the guilt hit her.

Sara stared at her, her blood pressure rising to a dangerous level. She should never have been put in this position, and yet here she was, sitting opposite her senior officer, who was having a meltdown for no reason other than the fact that her devious nature had been uncovered.

Price dropped her hands and wiped her eyes on a tissue. "Please forgive me. We can get past this, Sara. Who else knows?"

Sara leapt out of her seat and leaned over the desk, her face inches from Price's. "How dare you even suggest that?"

Rage guided her next move. She rang Carla. "Come to DCI Price's office and bring Barry with you."

"What? Why? Is something wrong?" Carla asked, sounding bemused.

"Do it!" Sara ended the call abruptly. "Look what you're doing to me. In all my years in the Force, I've never been this angry."

"Sara, don't do this. You won't be able to live with yourself... if you turn me in."

She rounded the desk, grabbed Price by the collar, yanked her boss to her feet and drew back her fist, ready to clobber her. The door burst open, and Carla yelled, "No!" it was enough to stop her.

"Sara, what the fuck is going on?" Carla's gaze flicked between Sara and Price, whom Sara had shoved away from her.

"She's the mole. She's been leaking information to Blake and Kline for years. She's the one who has consistently put Jessica's life in danger."

"No! She can't be," Carla shouted.

"Barry, slap the cuffs on her," Sara said. "I'm tempted to parade her around this station. Everyone and their dog should know what she's been up to."

"I can't believe what I'm hearing," Mary said from the doorway. "Chief, is this true?"

Price bowed her head in shame, which was enough to acknowledge her guilt.

The distraught secretary screamed and ran from the room.

"I believe everyone in this station will have the same reaction as your loyal secretary," Sara snarled. "I hope you're proud of yourself."

"I'm not. Don't do this to me. I'm begging you."

"If you hadn't risked an innocent woman's life this week, I might have been tempted to process you and be done with it. But I'm not prepared to let this lie. You deserve everything that's coming to you. Bent coppers need to be shown up for what they are... the lowest of the low in our society."

Barry assisted Price from her seat and slapped the handcuffs on. Then, the three of them took her downstairs where she was processed, arrested and thrown into a cell. To rot, for all Sara cared.

Her anger was vindicated when she received a call from the superintendent, congratulating her on a job well done. Her senior officer's blasé attitude rendered her speechless.

The station felt different now. Like something had shifted in its foundations. Sara walked through the halls, everyone's eyes on her. They all knew what had happened with Price, and though no one said it out loud, the trust in the department had been shaken.

Carla found her later that afternoon standing by the station's back entrance, staring out at the city. "Are you okay?"

Sara's breath shuddered when she exhaled. "I don't know. Part of me is glad it's over, but then... part of me is having trouble dealing with what Price did. She was supposed to protect us. Protect Jessica. And all this time, she was unforgivably feeding information to Blake."

Carla nodded and leaned against the wall beside her. "Yeah, it's a tough one. But you can't blame yourself for not seeing it. Price fooled everyone."

"I trusted her," Sara muttered. "I trusted her with everything."

"And she betrayed you. But that says more about her than you."

Sara was quiet for a moment, her thoughts tangled in a giant web.

"What happens now—with Price, I mean?" her partner asked.

"She's facing charges," Sara said quietly. "They'll almost certainly cut her a deal, considering the blackmail, but she won't be coming back."

Carla nodded.

Sara shuddered. The loss of Price was more than just the loss of her senior officer. It was the loss of a mentor, someone she had looked up to for years. "I keep thinking about what else Blake had on her," Sara said after a pause. "What could make someone like her turn so easily, apart from the debt she was in? Was it fear? Greed? Or something else?"

"We may never know. It seems unbelievable that it was only to do with the debt," Carla replied. "But you stopped it. You got Jessica back, and you arrested Blake. That's what matters."

Sara turned to face her, a small, tired smile tugging at the corners of her mouth. "No, we did. As a team, we did all that."

Carla grinned. "Now come on, we've got a pile of paperwork waiting for us. You know, just in case you thought being a hero meant you could get out of it."

Sara laughed softly, shaking her head as they walked back inside.

EPILOGUE

A few days later, Sara and Carla collected Daniel Harding and took him to meet his wife. Daniel was quiet during the journey, although he'd admitted to Sara when they'd picked him up that he was apprehensive about seeing his wife again after all she'd been through. Sara wanted to check in on Jessica one last time before the trial, to make sure she was really okay after the traumatic week she'd endured.

Jessica opened the door to what they regarded as the safe, safe house. She smiled when she saw Sara. But her smile slipped when Daniel peered over Sara's shoulder.

"Daniel, Sara, Carla," she whispered. "I wasn't expecting to see any of you."

"I wanted to see how you were doing," Sara replied, stepping inside. "How are you holding up?"

Daniel held out his arms to hug his wife. "I should have been there for you."

Jessica waved his apology away and kissed him on the cheek. Then she faced Sara and shrugged. "I'm okay. Better than I thought I'd be, considering everything that has happened."

"You've been through a lot," Sara said gently. "It's okay not to be okay, you know."

Jessica nodded, her eyes reflecting the ordeal that had blighted her life. "I know. I'm getting there. Knowing that Blake's in prison, that it's finally over... it helps." She held out her hand to Daniel.

Jessica led the four of them into the small living room and invited them to take a seat. Daniel sat on the sofa next to her, their hands tightly linked.

"I was terrified," Jessica admitted after a long pause. "When they took me the final time, I thought... it was the end. I thought I'd never see anyone again."

Sara swallowed hard, the memories of the week rushing through her mind. "I'm sorry we didn't get to you sooner."

Jessica reached out, placing a hand on Sara's arm. "You saved me, Sara. You and Carla. I don't know how to thank you for that."

"You don't have to thank us," Sara said. "We were just doing our job."

Jessica smiled softly, her eyes glistening with emotion. "It's more than that. You gave me my life back."

"I have some news that has devastated everyone who works at the station," Sara said.

Jessica tilted her head and asked, "What's that?"

"During the investigation, it came to light that a few moles were supplying Blake with the information about where you were."

"That's how they were able to get to me."

Sara nodded. "I'm so sorry, we're as shocked as you, especially when we found out that my immediate boss, DCI Price, was the main instigator."

Jessica gasped. "My God."

"What?" Daniel seethed. "I hope she's been arrested."

"She has. I can't apologise enough."

"It's not your fault, Sara," Jessica said. "You did your best with the odds stacked against you. I'm so grateful for you overcoming the adversity that blocked your path. Enough about that. When can I go home? That's if you want me back, Daniel?"

He kissed her on the lips to reassure her. "Goes without saying."

"Let's get the trial out of the way first. Judge Reynolds is pushing it through for us. There's talk that it could take place in a couple of weeks."

"Okay, at least we won't have to wait months for the ordeal to be over."

As Sara left the safe house, a sense of closure finally settled over her. The case was coming to an end, and Jessica would testify against Blake, ensuring that he and his evil network would never harm anyone again. The road ahead wouldn't be easy for Jessica, but she was strong, and Sara had no doubt that she and Daniel would get through it together.

Back at the station, Sara walked into the quiet of her office, the stress in her shoulders easing at last. The board had been taken down, the case files boxed up and, for the first time in what felt like forever, there was a sense of finality in the air.

She sat at her desk, letting out a long breath as she glanced at the stack of case files that had already begun to gather. There would always be another case, another mystery to solve. But, for now, she could let herself breathe, knowing that they had won this time.

Carla knocked on the door, leaning in with a grin. "Ready for the next one?"

Sara smiled, a lightness returning to her that she hadn't felt in weeks. "Yeah," she said, her voice steady. "I'm ready."

And as the day came to a close, Sara felt a renewed sense of purpose. They had fought hard and won, and while there would always be new battles to face—with the mystery of who the new DCI would be—she knew she had the strength to deal with what lay ahead.

In the end, that was what truly mattered.

THE END

. . .

THANK YOU FOR READING VANISHED, don't miss the next thrilling adventure in this series, Shadows of Deception.

WHILE I HAVE YOUR ATTENTION, have you read any of my other fast-paced crime thrillers yet?

WHY NOT TRY the first book in the award-winning Justice series, the first book is Cruel Justice

OR THE FIRST book in the spin-off Justice Again series,
    Gone in Seconds

MAYBE YOU'D PREFER my thriller series set in the stunning Lake District, the first book is To Die For

PERHAPS YOU'D PREFER to try one of my other police procedural series, the DI Kayli Bright series which begins with
    The Missing Children

OR MAYBE YOU'D enjoy the DI Sally Parker series set in Norfolk,
    Wrong Place

OR MY GRITTY police procedural starring DI Nelson set in Manchester, Torn Apart

. . .

OR MAYBE YOU'D like to try one of my successful psychological thrillers I know The Truth or She's Gone or Shattered Lives

ALSO BY M A COMLEY

Caring For Justice (a 24,000 word novella)

Savage Justice (a 17,000 word novella)

Justice at Christmas #2 (a 15,000 word novella)

Gone in Seconds (Justice Again series #1)

Ultimate Dilemma (Justice Again series #2)

Shot of Silence (Justice Again series #3)

Taste of Fury (Justice Again series #4)

Crying Shame (Justice Again series #5)

See No Evil (Justice Again series #6)

To Die For (DI Sam Cobbs #1)

To Silence Them (DI Sam Cobbs #2)

To Make Them Pay (DI Sam Cobbs #3)

To Prove Fatal (DI Sam Cobbs #4)

To Condemn Them (DI Sam Cobbs #5)

To Punish Them (DI Sam Cobbs #6)

To Entice Them (DI Sam Cobbs #7)

To Control Them (DI Sam Cobbs #8)

To Endanger Lives (DI Sam Cobbs #9)

To Hold Responsible (DI Sam Cobbs #10)

To Catch a Killer (DI Sam Cobbs #11)

To Believe the Truth (DI Sam Cobbs #12)

To Blame Them (DI Sam Cobbs 13)

To Judge Them (DI Sam Cobbs #14)

To Fear Him (DI Sam Cobbs #15)

To Deceive Them (DI Sam Cobbs #16)

Forever Watching You (DI Miranda Carr thriller)

Wrong Place (DI Sally Parker thriller #1)

No Hiding Place (DI Sally Parker thriller #2)

Cold Case (DI Sally Parker thriller#3)

Run for Your Life (DI Sara Ramsey #9)

Cold Mercy (DI Sara Ramsey #10)

Sign of Evil (DI Sara Ramsey #11)

Indefensible (DI Sara Ramsey #12)

Locked Away (DI Sara Ramsey #13)

I Can See You (DI Sara Ramsey #14)

The Kill List (DI Sara Ramsey #15)

Crossing The Line (DI Sara Ramsey #16)

Time to Kill (DI Sara Ramsey #17)

Deadly Passion (DI Sara Ramsey #18)

Son of the Dead (DI Sara Ramsey #19)

Evil Intent (DI Sara Ramsey #20)

The Games People Play (DI Sara Ramsey #21)

Revenge Streak (DI Sara Ramsey #22)

Seeking Retribution (DI Sara Ramsey #23)

Gone... But Where? (DI Sara Ramsey #24)

Last Man Standing (DI Sara Ramsey #25)

Vanished (DI Sara Ramsey #26)

Shadows of Deception (DI Sara Ramsey #27)

I Know The Truth (A Psychological thriller)

She's Gone (A psychological thriller)

Shattered Lives (A psychological thriller)

Evil In Disguise – a novel based on True events

Deadly Act (Hero series novella)

Torn Apart (Hero series #1)

End Result (Hero series #2)

In Plain Sight (Hero Series #3)

Double Jeopardy (Hero Series #4)

Criminal Actions (Hero Series #5)

Regrets Mean Nothing (Hero series #6)

Prowlers (Di Hero Series #7)

Sole Intention (Intention series #1)

Grave Intention (Intention series #2)

Devious Intention (Intention #3)

Cozy mysteries

Murder at the Wedding

Murder at the Hotel

Murder by the Sea

Death on the Coast

Death By Association

Merry Widow (A Lorne Simpkins short story)

It's A Dog's Life (A Lorne Simpkins short story)

A Time To Heal (A Sweet Romance)

A Time For Change (A Sweet Romance)

High Spirits

The Temptation series (Romantic Suspense/New Adult Novellas)

Past Temptation

Lost Temptation

Clever Deception (co-written by Linda S Prather)

Tragic Deception (co-written by Linda S Prather)

Sinful Deception (co-written by Linda S Prather)

KEEP IN TOUCH WITH M A COMLEY

Newsletter
http://smarturl.it/8jtcvv

BookBub
www.bookbub.com/authors/m-a-comley

Blog
http://melcomley.blogspot.com

Facebook Readers' Page
https://www.facebook.com/groups/2498593423507951

TikTok
https://www.tiktok.com/@melcomley

Printed in Dunstable, United Kingdom

63647189R00121